I0612272

Copyrighted Material

The Blood Oath of Blackbriar Academy copyright © 2019 by
Olivia Ash.
Covert art commissioned and owned by Wispvine Publishing
LLC.
Book design and layout copyright © 2019 by Wispvine Publishing
LLC.

www.wispvine.com

978-1-939997-94-4

1st Edition

BOOKS BY OLIVIA ASH

Dragon Dojo Brotherhood

Reign of Dragons

Fate of Dragons

Blood of Dragons

Age of Dragons

Fall of Dragons

Death of Dragons

War of Dragons

Queen of Dragons

Myths of Dragons

Vessel of Dragons

Gods of Dragons

A Legend Among Dragons

Blackbriar Academy

The Trials of Blackbriar Academy

The Shadows of Blackbriar Academy

The Hex of Blackbriar Academy

The Blood Oath of Blackbriar Academy

The Battle of Blackbriar Academy

The Nighthelm Guardian Series

City of the Sleeping Gods

City of Fractured Souls

City of the Enchanted Queen

Demon Queen Saga

Princes of the Underworld

Wars of the Underworld

Sentinel Saga

By Dahlia Leigh and Olivia Ash

The Shadow Shifter

Join the exclusive group where all the cool kids hang out… Olivia's secret club for cool ladies! Consider this your formal invitation to a world of hot guys, fun people, and your fellow book lovers. Olivia hangs out in this group all the time. She made the group specifically for readers like you to come together and share their lives and interests, especially regarding the hot guys from her novels.

Check it out! Everyone in there is amazing, and you'll fit right in.

https://www.facebook.com/groups/LilaJeanOliviaAsh/

Sign up for email alerts of new releases AND an exclusive bonus novella from the Nighthelm Guardian series, *City of the Rebel Runes*, the prequel to *City of Sleeping Gods* only available to subscribers.

https://wispvine.com/newsletter/olivia-ash-email-signup/

Enjoying the series? Awesome! Help others discover Blackbriar Academy by leaving a review at Amazon.

THE BLOOD OATH OF BLACKBRIAR ACADEMY

Agatha is up to something, and with a witch that powerful, you can bet it won't be good for me.

She's always wanted to dig her claws into Milo, and when he starts acting -- well, *odd* -- I can only assume her shiny new necklace has something to do with it. It reeks of enchantment, and as Milo gets lost in the depths of her spell, only I can save him.

Messing with me is one thing. But messing with my men? That's unforgivable.

One by one, my men are being removed from my life.

First Milo. Then, Gideon. Powerful people are behind this, pulling the strings on my life in an effort to take everything I love away.

Which means Soren and Jesse are next on this deadly hit list.

You mess with my men, you mess with me.

What the people hunting us don't realize is you *don't* want to mess with *me*.

The people after us want war.

Well, I can give them *that*.

Ready or not, here I come.

THE BLOOD OATH OF BLACKBRIAR ACADEMY

BOOK FOUR OF THE BLACKBRIAR ACADEMY SERIES

OLIVIA ASH

CONTENTS

CHAPTER ONE

S weat beads along my skin as I move with much more grace than ever before.

In the years that I have been training, I only get better, and that shows as I continue to dodge every fist and block every kick. Even my magic responds quicker. My shield deflects powerful bursts of fire and light, and I deliver some devastating blasts myself.

Soren tries to pin me down, and I quickly backflip out of his grip, landing on my feet, crouching low, eyes zeroed in on his every move so that I can prepare for his next attack. The sun is just starting to rise over the horizon of the deserted beach we are training on, and I catch a very distracting, beautiful glimpse of the sands starting to turn red along the edge of the water.

It's almost mesmerizing how the light glitters off the tiny grains like rubies.

Now I see why this place is called Crimson Isles. It's fitting.

As a way to end the summer with a bang, Soren brought me back to Crimson Isles. My last visit didn't go so well, with the run-in with my aunt and her two goons, cutting my time here short. I'm happy to say that this visit trumps the last by a long shot.

My momentary distraction is enough for Soren to instantly take advantage as he kicks my feet out from under me. The world blurs around me in an array of color and light, until I'm on my back, staring at a wisp of cloud floating along the lightening blue sky. Soren appears in my vision, a satisfied smirk toying with his lips.

I playfully glare at him. "Cheater."

He quirks an eyebrow. "Is that so?"

I fight the smile tugging on my lips as he pulls himself over me, straddling me in the most delightful way. My body instantly burns with desire, and I decide to milk this for all it's worth.

After all, this is the first time in what seems like forever I'm training with Soren. Soon, classes will begin again as I enter my third year at Blackbriar

Academy, and that means time with him will be precious little.

As he leans in, amber eyes darkening as his focus moves to my lips, I bite the corner of my lower lip and buck. His eyes widen as he shoots over me, rolling in the sand. I quickly roll and climb to my feet with a triumphant smile. A chuckle leaves my lips.

"Is this really how you wanna play?" he asks.

I don't answer. Instead, I *charge*.

I'm not done with training yet. And with tight formation, we dance in the sand, fists flying, feet kicking, and the both of us dodging every blow as though we rehearsed this little routine dozens of times. Magic blasts hit the sand, sending bright red lights into the air like tiny magical fireworks.

It's beautiful.

And it just keeps getting *better*.

The more I train with Soren, the more I feel recharged, refueled, renewed. Even despite my lack of sleep.

Since defeating my aunt at the Blackwood family estate, I'm haunted by nightmares. The shadows of my otherwise sunny life. Dreams of not saving my father in time, losing one or more of my men in the fight, of failing to protect the ones I love.

A chill prickles my skin along my arms, and I press

my lips firmly together to force the shadows of my terrors at bay, swinging harder, moving faster, keeping up with Soren and nearly besting him.

I smile, relishing in that feeling of what it would mean to best a man like Soren.

I catch his gaze, and there's a questioning behind his eyes that nearly takes my focus away. Nearly. But doesn't. I've grown beyond the simple distractions that would once land me on my back and him standing over me victorious.

That thought brings a new thrill to my senses, filling me with fluttering joy.

The sun rises higher into the sky, igniting the rest of the sands in glowing red and it's brilliant, magical, amazing.

I freaking love it.

The view is not only a wonder to take in, but it symbolizes so much for me. The beauty of what lies ahead of me. The power that I am unfolding and mastering as the days pass. The things that are yet to come. The promise of a better future.

A better me.

And *that* renews my faith in myself.

No one can take my power away from me. I won't let them.

I will stop anyone who tries.

A strange shadow hovers over us, and Soren instantly shields me. "Duck!"

"Why?" I ask as I'm nearly forced to my knees under the pressure of Soren's abrupt act of protection.

Flapping fills the air, followed by a loud screech that shakes me to the core, and fills the pit of my stomach with a heavy weight. Whatever this is, it's big, and it doesn't sound friendly.

Soren lifts from me and faces the creature as I climb to my feet and do the same. I freeze in place, shocked by the creature sitting in front of me, preening its feathers as if dropping in front of two unsuspecting humans is an everyday occurrence. The large bird gazes at us with its storm grey eyes. Its ash-colored beak tilts downward and makes a low clicking sound, but the bird remains in place. It watches us with an air of curiosity. A crown of feathers adorns the back of his head, and I instantly feel a pull to pet it through whatever enchantment this bird possesses.

I take an unconscious step forward. Soren's hand grips my arm and holds me back. I meet his gaze. His expression is a mixture of fight-mode and caution.

"What is it?" I ask.

"Harpy eagle. He's young, judging by his size, and possibly feral." He keeps his amber eyes on the giant creature as he speaks with a low, even tone.

"I've never seen one before. He's beautiful."

Soren's grip tightens on my arm as he pulls me back. "He's dangerous."

"Why? Because you think he's feral?" I level my gaze on his. "How do you know?"

"I'll explain later. Right now, we need to get as far away from him as possible, and hope that we don't set him off."

I laugh. "What is he going to do? Peck us to death?"

I joke, but it's only because Soren being this serious unsettles me, and I don't like it one bit.

He finally meets my gaze. "Far worse. These birds are storm wielders."

"Oh. They're magical?" I take in the bird with his dark grey and white feathers, and it makes sense. He would blend into a storm easily. He holds an enchantment that makes me want to get closer. Sort of like unsuspecting prey.

Soren growls. "The only thing more dangerous than a harpy eagle is a feral or untrained one."

I look at the bird again, wondering how in the world Soren could make that assessment of the creature standing at my height. It doesn't look dangerous. But, ultimately, I know better than to doubt Soren. If he says it's unsafe, then it is.

The bird stares at us curiously for a few more

seconds and makes a high-pitched purring sound. Goosebumps prickle along my skin as the hairs on the back of my neck and along my arms stand on end. The air fills with static as the bird sets his eyes on us with clear intent, and I suddenly don't want to be anywhere near this storm-wielding creature.

"Get your shield ready." Soren's voice is full of warning.

With a nod and a flick of my wrist, it's up. The bird opens his beak and the electric blue of lightning glows at the back of his throat. I barely have time to blink as a bolt shoots toward us. As the powerful hit slams into my shield, I'm pushed back, my feet sliding through the sand. Bits and pieces of the grains spill into my shoes.

Soren rushes forward, throwing ropes of fire toward the bird. One burning strand smacks the creature in his face. He squawks indignantly and takes flight as the smell of burning flesh and feathers fills the air. Winds kick up, spraying my face with sand, stinging and nipping like tiny needles stabbing my cheeks and arms. Bringing my shield closer to me, I angle it just slightly above me to help protect my skin and stop the onslaught.

As the harpy eagle takes flight, steel grey clouds

gather above us in the sky. The air rumbles and warms, filling with even more static.

It's very clear to me now why Soren was so on guard with the creature. Just a baby, and it's creating quite a mess for us. Not to mention a challenge. If he climbs too high, we're done for.

"How do you kill it?" I shout over the winds and booming thunder.

"Fire."

"Good luck. The wind is too strong!"

I peek over my shield and notice the bird is no longer climbing into the air but hovering a good fifty feet above us. He shrieks out a loud call, and I sense he is trying to find backup.

That is simply something I can't allow to happen.

As Soren struggles to blast the bird with fire magic, I feel something icy flow through me. It's unique enough that it differs from the sensation I get with Milo. It's so much stronger, and my muscles ache with the feeling.

Trusting my gut, I lower my shield enough to aim my open hand toward the bird, and my magic responds in a rush of ice from my palm. The cold blast smacks into the bird, and it falters in the air. Shards break off, blowing in the wind, darting off toward Soren like frozen arrows.

"Shit. Watch out!"

Too late.

Soren already saw them coming, barely moving in time to avoid being impaled. A shard grazes his leg, leaving a nasty gash in his left calf. He glares at me. I shrug. Yeah, that was close, but the move worked. The harpy eagle's wings are coated in heavy ice, too much for him to keep afloat. He angrily cries out as he fights to stay in the air. But it's no use. He slowly descends to the ground.

As the creature lands, he uses his beak to peck at the ice covering his wings. The storm releases its angry torrential rains, and the winds continue to grow as the bird grows angry over not being able to fly.

Soren calls forth his magic, coaxing the flames dancing in his adept hands. But with all the wind and rain, his point about killing it with fire is proving to be easier said than done. A blast of wind knocks him to the ground. He grits his teeth in pain, undoubtedly from the icicle gash in his leg.

I keep an eye on the harpy eagle, ready to aim and fire my own blasts to cover Soren, but the wind that keeps knocking against me is only moving me farther away from the fight. If I am going to be helpful, I have to get rid of the wind resistance. But getting rid of my shield presents its own fair share of problems.

There will be no protection against the wind, sand, rain, or the bird.

Keeping the shield just isn't an option. Not if I want Soren to live through this without becoming harpy eagle fodder.

With a frustrated sigh, I let go of my shield and am instantly blasted with the full force of the wind and rain. I feel like I'm being pelted with fist blows, the way the elements combine and fall down on me.

Holy hell this hurts.

Storm-wielder is an understatement. This bird is seriously a beast with its magic.

Through the painful onslaught of the magical storm, with lightning blasting the ground every few seconds, I notice the ice is melting from the rain and the last chunk keeping the beast grounded is almost removed.

We most definitely can't let him get airborne again.

I suck in a quick breath and ignore the stabbing, prickly rain hitting my body. I aim my hand again, but then hold back—it's too risky. I can't afford injuring Soren again, accident or no. The air is now super-charged. I already know that means lightning. And if this bird can give me a beating with its powers of wind and rain, I certainly don't want to stick around to get struck by lightning.

Soren's already back on his feet and manages to land a decent blast of fire to the bird, and for a few precious seconds, the storm subsides. I push through the pain and rush toward the bird, right palm facing the creature, as icy magic flows through my veins and fills my arm. I quickly form a wall of ice around the giant creature, topping it off with a ceiling to keep him from flying away.

Soren gazes at me with an expression of approval and pride. I smile.

"Nice."

I shrug. "That's a good word for it." I shake out my arms to release the remnants of numbing cold still filling them.

He faces the creature still trapped within my ice blockade. His hands power up with a brilliant orange fire, and before I can ask if it will penetrate my ice wall, I get my answer. Soren sends a final blast of fire that ploughs through the frozen barrier and straight to the harpy eagle's chest. The creature lets out a final shriek before the light fades from its storm grey eyes.

As the silence settles between us, both of us working to catch our breath, alarms ring through the air in the distance.

"Magusari," Soren says.

I nod.

"They'll take care of the bird and escort us to the citadel for questioning."

"Are we in trouble?" I ask with a quirked eyebrow.

He shakes his head as he studies the bird. "No. Formalities. Like us, they will want to know how a harpy eagle got onto the island and who's responsible."

Ah. Makes sense.

CHAPTER TWO

The med ward within the citadel looks more like a spa than a clinical room. It's housed in the belly of the castle-like structure, with sandstone arches and floors. A large rug takes up the center of the room with candles sitting on shelves that line the walls. The candles' flames flicker with an iridescence that makes it obvious they're enchanted. As I breathe in the soft, slightly musky scent of the candles, my aches and pains fade a little.

I sit at the edge of a cushy bed, giving the nurse a nod of thanks as she finishes wrapping up my bruised arms in salve-soaked bandages. A soothing warmth penetrates my skin.

"You can take it off once you feel it cool down," the white-haired nurse says with a smile. She throws me a bemused look when Soren hisses and grunts from across the room. Another nurse has him sitting on an examination table as she stitches up the gash on his leg.

I smirk, knowing that he wouldn't dare be caught yelling out in pain in front of us.

The thud of heavy boots catches my attention and I turn toward the magusari captain entering the ward. He stands off to the side until the elderly nurse excuses herself. He closes the gap between us, and I sigh inwardly, resigned to the fact that I'll have to speak with him first, though I knew nothing about harpy eagles until today.

He has all the seriousness that Soren carries with him constantly but has crow's feet that crease the corners of his brilliant blue eyes and laugh lines around his full lips. His skin is smooth and the color of chocolate. A thin layer of facial hair is perfectly sculpted into a well-manicured beard. He's quite handsome, and I can tell he's in detective mode with the way a crease pulls his eyebrows together as he scribbles away on his notepad. But clearly, he knows how to have fun as well.

"Ms. Blackwood, I'm Captain Lionel Rhodes. I believe one of my colleagues took down your initial statement?"

I nod, then squeeze my eyes momentarily to block out flashes of the encounter running through my mind. Of how my initial sense of wonder and awe quickly turned to wariness, and how our beach-side sparring turned into a magical brawl. Apparently with a creature that didn't even belong here. It really is as big of a deal as Soren made it out to be.

"They're dangerous creatures," the captain says. "You are both lucky to have escaped without life-threatening injuries."

"That's what I said," Soren adds. He winces as his nurse continues to work.

The captain shakes his head. "Do you recall any other harpies nearby?"

"No," I say. "He was alone. What caused him to come so close to us?"

"Make sure you emphasize in your report that it was young," Soren adds. "It doesn't make sense to have just one so young out this far alone." Soren hisses and glares at the nurse that twists the lid on some salve she just placed on his wound.

If she's in the least bothered by Soren's anger, she doesn't show it. The fact that she isn't reacting to him seems to make him even more disgruntled. I chuckle under my breath.

"I agree, Mr. McCallister." The captain taps his pen

against his chin and looks to be in deep thought. "The farms raising them know there are heavy penalties for strays and ferals. The fact that it was roaming free means it escaped from its farm before being registered or tagged."

I scoot back a little on the plush bed and cross my legs beneath me. "And you think there could be more?"

"For everyone's sake, I hope not." The captain slides his notepad and pen into a side pocket. "There are only two farms in the U.S. that raise harpy eagles, but something tells me that both of them will deny ownership of that feral one. Is there anything else you can think of that would help?"

"I don't think so." I look to Soren for confirmation. He is still busy glaring at the nurse who won't show him an ounce of fear or remorse.

My kind of gal.

"Stay off your feet for at least five minutes, Mr. McCallister. I'll be back to check the bandage and dismiss you both." Her voice is polite, but firm. She sets her emerald gaze on me with a nod and knowing smile before walking out of the room.

"Any questions for me?" Captain Rhodes asks.

"I have one," Soren says as he hops from the examination table and gently puts weight on his leg. With a shrug, he joins me at the bed, facing the captain. "Why now?"

"So much for staying put," I say.

Soren ignores my comment, keeping his attention on the other man.

He shakes his head. "That's what we hope to uncover. For now, I'll organize a hunt and send an investigator out to the farm closest to us to see if they have noticed a missing eaglet."

"Exactly how close is this farm?" I ask, not bothering to hide the displeasure in my voice.

The captain sets his gaze on me. "We've got this under control. Don't worry."

"And the body?" Soren asks.

"We'll test the carcass to make sure he wasn't experiencing any unusual diseases or curses. Then, he'll be incinerated."

"So…" I drag out the word. "It's not all that common to run into these birds?"

"Not by chance, no. The last known reported attack was over one hundred fifty years ago. Control of the population was in its infant stages back then. You've seen what one eaglet can do. A roaming group of them would be devastating to mage and human communities alike. The creature had to have come from one of the farms. Seeing as how the northwestern farm isn't likely, we will be searching the one in the southeast."

I nod. Good information. I'll drill Soren for more when Captain Rhodes leaves. He has an investigation to get to and all.

"For now, I ask that the two of you keep the incident to yourselves. We have the people here pacified, but we wouldn't want the information getting out and causing a widespread panic." The captain turns to Soren. "I'll send you a report of our findings once it's complete."

"Thank you, Captain."

He bows in reverence to Soren, who still remains an elite ranking officer of the magusari. Facing me, he nods once and turns on his heels and heads out the arched doorway. As soon as he is gone, I turn to Soren. "Spill everything."

He sighs and leans against the side of the bed and crosses his arms over his chest. "What do you want to know?"

"If harpy eagles are so dangerous, why are there two farms filled with them in the States? How does that work exactly?"

"Carefully."

I quirk an eyebrow, waiting for him to continue. When he doesn't, I add, "Obviously."

"They are a very aggressive, easily angered breed, but they do serve a purpose for mages. I know, it seems crazy, especially since they're known to sometimes carry off full-grown men when their normal prey is otherwise unavailable. They're dangerous because of their storm magic, as you found out."

"Uh huh, but there are two farms. Why?"

He holds up his middle and index fingers. "I'll give you two reasons. One is to keep the population in check. The other is because the families that care for them are experts in grooming and training them. Feral ones are of no use and dangerous."

"Training? For what?" I lean forward, a frown pulling at my lips.

"Think of them as giant magical Rottweilers."

"So, they're like guard dogs?"

"In essence. Rich mage families purchase them for private security. Some have even obtained eagles trained well enough to accompany hunting parties." He runs his hands through his hair. "It's one thing to ensure they don't harm people, but using them as glorified pets… it's monstrous."

"Sounds like a horrible fate for such majestic creatures."

"I wish there was a better solution, but these aren't exactly the type of creatures you let roam free." He levels his gaze on me, and I almost shrink back with the heat of anger burning in his darkened amber eyes. I didn't expect him to display that amount of passion over this.

In the end, I square my shoulders. "We should help, if we can. We were the only witnesses to that feral one."

He shakes his head. "Let the magusari take care of it. Besides, I had other plans for us, and we still have time."

"What plans?" I roll my eyes. "Please, not another surprise. Haven't we learned our lesson about those?"

He chuckles as he stands straight and holds out his hand toward me. "Trust me, you'll love this one."

I take his hand and ham up a groan. But I can't help the smile that comes to my face.

Before long, we are back outside and walking through the more familiar section of Crimson Isles, and I realize exactly where we are heading.

"We're going to see my father?"

"Don't ruin it," he mutters with a smile, clearly giving it all away.

I poke him in the ribs. "I planned on making a stop to see him before we left anyway."

"To see how he's settling into his new life?" He glances at me sideways and I'm caught by the gentle quirk in the corner of his lips that gives me an idea for a little pit-stop.

"That, and to just visit with him. He may have a new identity, but he's still my father."

Once my father was fully recovered, he and Gideon devised a plan to help him start a new life where he could be helpful but keep a low profile. He now operates under a disguise and lives in a very luxurious apartment on the Isles.

Within moments, we're at his door, waiting for him to answer. And when he does, I throw myself into his arms and hug him tightly. The disguise will take a little getting used to. Shaggy, shoulder-length hair has replaced his short cut, and there are wrinkles that weren't there before, as well as a different shape to his nose. I know it's him though. The eyes say it all.

"Wren. Soren. What a pleasant surprise!"

"Thought we'd stop in and see how you are holding up." Soren shakes his hand.

Once securely inside the apartment, my father leads us to his study where a large cherry oak desk sits dead center, covered in papers, organized documents, notes, and even a few sheets of blueprints.

"All of these things were stored in strategic places when I was on the run. It's going to help me tremendously when the time comes."

"Dad, stop portaling around to old hiding places. You run the risk of getting caught." I chide him gently, but if I'm being honest, I'm rather proud. My father is fearless, smart, and forward thinking. I see where I get it from. Though it does bother me that he risks his identity each time he does it, I do have to admire his spunk. He's come so far since his captivity with the Order and has recovered fully from even Aunt Patricia's house. Once he was safe, he made enormous leaps and bounds in his recovery.

He chuckles. "I'm fine. See?"

I smile and nod, but I'm not willing to let him win this one completely. "For now."

He gestures to the papers collected on his desk. "The Order is after you and your magic. I'm not going to just sit around and twiddle my thumbs. The information I have stored away could prove to be useful in keeping you safe. No amount of risk is worth avoiding that."

"We all appreciate your help," Soren adds. "Wren does have a point. There is a moment where the risk becomes too great."

My father nods in agreement, his long greying beard bouncing with the movement. It's neat, actually, there's a large darker upside-down triangle that sits directly beneath the center of his bottom lip. His long, curly salt and pepper hair brushes against his shoulders in near perfect ringlets. The disguise even gave him darker skin. It's odd to see him in this disguise, but I'm glad he committed to it so deeply.

Other than insisting on gathering old intel from around the country, he's safe. And that's what counts.

Before long, we are on the balcony, eating roasted chicken and potatoes, watching the sun set over the town.

"I heard the sirens earlier, do you know what was going on? Got anything to do with the bandages you seem to not want to tell me about?" my father asks.

Soren finishes his bite and washes it back with a sip of wine. "Wren and I were attacked by a harpy eagle on the beach. It was a young one, and wasn't tagged."

"Besides," I add, "the magusari are taking care of it."

He sets his fork on his plate and uses his napkin to dab at his face as he nods. Once finished, he looks at me and says, "Though the magusari are a capable force," he nods toward Soren who nods in return, "it is still wise to keep a look out."

"Why?" I ask, eyebrows pulling together.

"Because," Soren answers, "if there is one, there is always others."

My father nods. "That's right. There are always more, whether you know about them or not."

That explains why the bird was desperately calling for help before. I bite the corner of my lower lip.

"There's something else you want to say, but you're not?" I ask, noticing the thoughts crossing my father's eyes.

He shakes his head. "I don't think it was an accident. In fact, I'm almost one hundred percent sure it wasn't."

"We'll keep an eye out," Soren promises.

My father sets his gaze on Soren. "Just be careful. I wouldn't engage these birds if I could help it."

I set my eyes to the sky, carefully gleaning from the cloudy night any movement or shadows that don't belong. I don't see any, but one thing is for certain—if my father is worried, begging caution on our parts, then there is a reason. And a very good one.

CHAPTER THREE

I sit on the edge of a cliff in one of my favorite gardens, overlooking the ocean that surrounds Blackbriar. Mermaids splash about below, glancing at me every once in a while, more accepting of my presence than gazing curiously at me.

The memory of my encounter with them during the trials remains fresh at the forefront of my mind. I shudder at how close they were to claiming me.

As I shove that thought away, I look around for Savannah. I haven't seen her all summer, and to be perfectly frank, that worries me. No word from her makes me wonder if something horrible has happened, and I can't let myself get caught in that sticky web.

The wait isn't unpleasant, anyway.

Soft clouds float along the deep blue sky, reflecting in the ocean like a mirror. And the sun graces my skin with its comforting warmth. I've been here for hours hoping to bump into Savannah. I don't even know when she will arrive. I stopped by her room on the way to this place and one of her housemates said she hadn't arrived yet. I can't shake the concern gnawing at me.

Just as I'm about to give up and head inside, cool pulsing flows through me. Without turning my head to look, I smile. "Hey, Jesse."

"Clearly I need to up my game if you can tell it's me before I allow it." He sits next to me and bumps his shoulder against mine. I smile at him as he looks toward the base of the cliff, gazing at the mermaids.

I laugh. "Oh, Jesse. How I've missed you."

"Naturally. I'm adorable."

More peals of laughter bubble out of me and this is exactly what I needed. Once the laughing spell releases me, I lean into him, resting my head on his shoulder and sliding an arm through his. "How was your summer?"

"Dismal." His voice comes out more light than disappointed. "Yours?"

"Interesting."

"How so?" He asks, tucking a strand of copper hair behind my ear.

"Uh-uh. You first. How did it go with your siblings?"

"You just had to bring *those* two up?" He playfully glares at me as I look up at him.

I shrug. "So?"

"Other than going through a grand total of three nannies this summer, they're great."

"Oh gods. Why?"

He gives me a "really?" look. "They seem to have a knack for over-the-top pranks and have essentially beat their record of nannies quitting on them in the course of three months. I would feel sorry for my dad for having to go through the process of hiring another, but he's occupied himself with other pursuits recently."

The way he speaks of his father has me wondering how okay Jesse really is. It seems like him and his dad are at odds. "What do you mean?"

I hope my question doesn't come off as prying, but I don't really get to see the serious side of Jesse often, and I want to be here for him if he needs me to be.

He stands up and paces, shoulders rigid as his breaths turn ragged. "While my mother remains holed up in a home, mind unthreaded and unaware of the world around her, my father decided to fall in love with someone else. He's betrayed her."

I stand up and take a step toward him until I realize that he needs to vent, not be coddled. Staying put, I let him get his feelings out.

He shakes his head as he faces me. "It's not right!"

I nod. "I'm sorry, Jesse. What can I do to help?"

"Nothing. I've tried it all. Even got my brothers to help. But it's no use. He's in love with her. Even showed me the ring he's planning on giving her. Even went as far as to tell me my mom is permanently mentally incapacitated and never coming back, and that a judge agreed. Then he said she would want him to move on, and me and my brothers too."

I nod. I do understand where Jesse is coming from. It's an unfortunate situation that no one can do anything about now. I can tell this is twisting Jesse's heart and soul. He's loyal, dedicated, devoted. I would worry if this didn't upset him.

Jesse's pacing stops and he stands with his back to me, struggling to maintain his composure. I take that as my cue and close the gap between us, wrapping my arms around him from behind and resting my head on his back. "We'll get through this. Your dad obviously believes your mother is gone and he wants to rebuild his life. I don't agree with how he's doing it, but we can't control his decisions. I will still help you do whatever we can to help your mom."

His hands cover my arms and he leans into me ever so slightly. "I'm torn between feeling sympathy toward my father who spent all these years depressed and alone, and loyalty toward my mother. It's not like she's dead."

"I know." I lean closer into him.

"And this woman is truly a force. Especially as she's won my brothers over. With their pranks. She joins them. I haven't seen them this happy in years."

At least he sounds calmer now. That's something.

"And you?"

He shrugs. "I'm happy that they're happy, but I still need to help my mom, even if the world thinks she will never recover her mind."

"Good."

He twists in my arms and rests his cheek on the top of my head. "So, about your interesting summer."

I sigh. "I fought off a harpy eagle with Soren. That basically ends the interesting and exciting bits. Not much else to talk about unless you want to hear about my trainings."

He chuckles and the sound makes me smile. "Sounds like something you and Soren would get into. I'm glad you're okay. Now, how about we do a little training of our own?" His hands slide lower down my back to my ass, pushing me into his growing erection stretching the crotch of his pants.

I smack him. "You're horrible."

"Or maybe, I just know what I like and what I want." He kisses me, and it's hot and heavy. I pull away as laughter bubbles between our lips.

"Behave yourself, and maybe I'll sleep in your room tonight." I add a wink for fun and put a little distance between us.

He groans and charges. Smiling, I take off running in circles, avoiding his grasp. It's fun and lighthearted, and exactly what we needed.

He finally catches me, and we fall to the ground. Once the world stops spinning, we spend a few moments catching our breath. I watch the clouds, and as the moment of fun fades, the worry for my friend becomes more prominent.

"What's wrong?" Jesse asks.

"Have you seen Savannah?"

"Not yet. Why?"

"She's usually here by now. I just have a bad feeling something is up."

He pulls me into him, the grass squeals with the movement. I chuckle as I lean into him. He kisses the side of my head. "That girl can come back from the most tragic of circumstances. Trust me, she will be here. And I know you'll catch up."

"Yeah." I smile. "You're right. She's a firecracker."

"Indeed." He squeezes me to him a little more. "All in due time, my love. Things will fall into place."

I find such immense comfort in Jesse's arms that I become lost in the peacefulness of lying with him on the grass, staring at the clouds as they move over the island. This may not be the idea I had in mind when I came out to my favorite spot, but it certainly is a beautiful, relaxing time to share with him.

CHAPTER FOUR

I walk into my first official class of my third year at Blackbriar Academy with my head held high. It's almost hard to believe it's been two years since I first came to the school for my trials. I'm empowered by the changes I've gone through. I am loving my magic, my men, and who I'm becoming.

The level of control I've learned speaks volumes about my personal strength. I really don't think I could have done this all on my own though. Thankfully, I have my sexy men to support me through all this. I stride with confidence through my classroom as I spot Jesse, Milo, and Savannah sitting together. Joy flutters in my chest as I watch them chatting at a tall rectangular table with a sink and Bunsen burners. Among those are hot plates, test tube racks, glass stirrers, and multiple-sized flasks. Savannah's violet eyes meet mine, and she smiles.

Letting out a sigh of relief, I join her as she stands from her seat and wraps me into a big hug.

"There's my bestie," she says, her voice filled with that bubbly personality I've been missing.

I chuckle, wrapping my arms around her in our little awkward hug. "Bout time I got to see you. Thought something bad happened."

She gently pulls away. "I'll catch you up on the details later."

I smile. "I'm going to hold you to that."

She winks with a smirk and I take a seat at our table, smack dab in between Milo and Jesse. Milo grins at me and pushes his glasses farther up his nose.

Damn, I love my sexy nerd.

"Hey, you."

"Hey," he says.

"What have you been up to?" I ask.

He shrugs casually. "This and that."

Being coy, are we? I smile and nudge him a little. He looks like he wants to say more but is holding back for some reason. I study him for a moment longer and decide he'll tell me when he's ready.

I look around the room and notice eight other tables with the same setup and four students sitting at each, talking among themselves as we wait for the professor to show up. Plastered to the dark grey walls are posters of alchemy scholars with famous sayings that glitter and glow, almost as if the words hover over the poster instead of being printed on them.

The wall to my left has floor to ceiling windows, painted with famous battles of the past, plants that have roots reaching into the crystal-filled ground, and an image of the island. I am caught by the beauty of them and feel like they could come to life at any moment. Because here at Blackbriar Academy, everything is magical. And I've learned to make it part of my life.

Jesse pokes me in the ribs. "How am I doing? Well, I'm glad you asked. My lady is sitting next to me now, so I'm fantastic."

I shake my head and roll my eyes. "Good to know."

"My sentiments exactly." He winks, and I clench my thighs as warmth pools between them.

He certainly knows how to get to me. Delightful tease that he is.

"Get a room," Savannah playfully chides.

I chuckle. "Don't help him with ideas."

"No, I actually like that one," Jesse adds.

I twist in my seat and face Milo. "So, had a good summer?"

He nods. "I have a lot to tell you once we have time."

"I'm looking forward to it."

He half-smiles in his bashful way and my heart flutters in my chest. My Milo. Please never lose that adorable sense of wonder in you.

A small, handheld brass bell lifts from the desk sitting dead center at the front of the class and hovers into the air, glittering with gold and silver. It rings, the sound chiming through the air, silencing all the talking as each student looks to see what the noise was for. My attention is drawn to a beautiful woman who looks to be around my age, standing tall and proud as she materializes at the head of the classroom. Her long brown hair flows along her shoulders as she shifts her piercing emerald gaze along the students in the classroom.

I gulp.

A series of gasps fills the room.

I'm still convinced being amazingly beautiful is a pre-requisite for being at this academy. Hands down, she's drop dead gorgeous. Sighs and ah's ripple silently through the room as everyone takes in our professor.

"Good morning, I'm Professor Crosswell. I specialize in poisons, potions, cures, and protections. With that in mind, I'll be teaching you practical applications of magic, and for our first week, we will be studying various curses and spells along with how to break them."

Murmurs fill the room. I look over my shoulder and notice several of the men in the room practically drooling, while some of the more self-conscious women covertly fiddle with their clothes and hair. I don't blame them. I'm fighting the urge to squirm.

There's quite a few of us in this laboratory-like room. I wonder if this is a mixed year class.

The professor snaps her fingers and textbooks appear in front of each of us, shimmering to life.

"A few rules before we begin..." She takes a deep breath, pausing to look over the faces waiting patiently for her to start. "I will not give you the answers. I will, however, give you the tools you need and help you find the answers. Life won't hand you the perfect remedy to the problems you'll face in the future, and neither will I. However, you can and will learn where to look for solutions and how to implement them. And it is my job to teach you where to look."

"Great," Jesse leans in and whispers to me. "I had a math teacher who said the same thing—I failed the class."

I shush him and cover my mouth with the back of my hand to stifle my chuckle.

Professor Crosswell's gaze sweeps across the room, as if already judging who will succeed and who will barely make it through with a passing grade. "This is my style of teaching, and through getting things wrong initially, you would better learn what to do right. That is not to say that I am unavailable when I'm needed. My obligation is to ensure your safety and wellbeing while you are in my classroom. If something goes awry, or if someone is bleeding from the eyes, I'll aid in those moments. Dire circumstances only."

"I like her already," Jesse says with a smirk.

Milo scribbles the highlights of Crosswell's pep talk in his notebook. "I agree, this is the best way to learn. Trial and error."

"I don't have a good track record with trial and error," I mutter.

Savannah snorts. "Have faith in yourself. You're better at it than you think."

I glance at Savannah as she starts flipping through the pages of the book.

I suck in a deep breath and pull the textbook to me. Flipping open the cover, I rake my gaze along the numerous passages of the introduction and notice that the professor authored this work.

For someone who doesn't want to give us all the answers, she certainly has everything spelled out for us in these pages. At least, that's what it seems.

"Who can tell me what the most common characteristics of a poisoning are?" Professor Crosswell asks.

Savannah's hand shoots into the air.

"Miss Fey?"

Savannah takes a deep breath. "Most poisonings present with very specific characteristics. Very few present differently. As such, all of them have symptoms of fever, rash, paleness, and so on."

"Excellent." She smiles. "Family training?"

Savannah nods. "Yes, I come from a long line of healers. I help my father and brothers work potions for cures quite a bit."

"You are a step ahead of most. Good job." Professor Crosswell searches the faces in the room. She rests on mine briefly, a hint of knowing in her eyes that makes me a little uncomfortable, before she moves on to other students. "And what about curses?"

Jesse elbows me in the side. "I've got this," he says in a low voice as he lifts his hand.

"Yes, Mr. Taylor?"

He smirks. "Like with poisons, curses have typical symptoms such as insomnia, paranoid delusions, hallucinations, lack of appetite, skin discoloration, and any combination thereof."

The professor seems slightly taken aback by Jesse's response. "Where does your experience come from, dare I ask?"

"My twin brothers." His voice comes out matter-of-factly, and I glance at him with questioning. He meets my gaze and winks.

"How unfortunate."

He shrugs. "Mostly entertaining, actually." He leans in a little closer. "I got them back by selling all their video games and putting the money up where they will never find it."

The professor frowns and looks to the rest of the class. "How about discovering poison and deciphering which cure to use?"

I lean closer to Jesse. "I don't think she likes your response."

"She's apparently never had twin brothers who love pranks."

Another student in the class responds to the professor. A guy with a tenor voice that carries across the room, though he's tucked away in the far back corner. "Depending on what symptoms are present, there could be a handful of poisons. Looking deeper into those options will generally point to the right cure."

"And for curses?" The professor asks. "Mr. Taylor, you seem to have lengthy experience in this department. Any knowledge to share with your classmates?"

He leans forward. "Unlike poisons, curses don't have a list of simple cures on hand. Lifting a curse takes much more time, resources, and effort. Why? Because, like my brothers, people can come up with the most creative ways to torture others."

She frowns again.

I poke Jesse's side. "You may want to stop sharing now."

He shrugs. "I'm just getting started." A devilish smile pulls on his lips. I shake my head. He's digging himself a hole. I should probably get him a shovel.

"Then, how would you reverse a curse?" Professor Crosswell's pointed gaze warns Jesse against giving another flippant anecdote.

"With luck, which I'm fortunate to have a fair share in, the trick is figuring out the intention. All curses are specific, meant to harm someone in a particular way for a purpose. From there, you can unravel the threads, one by one, until you have yourself a fully reversed curse."

"And if that doesn't work?" She asks.

"My condolences." Jesse's eyes darken, and there's not an ounce of joking within his voice, which makes a pinch form in the center of my forehead. I have a feeling he's referring to his mother. My heart breaks for him.

Professor Crosswell clears her throat. "And poisons? Miss Fey, would you like to share?"

She nods. "I would love to. Apothecaries carry premade antidotes for the most common and some of the most complex poisons. Healers sometimes carry much smaller stocks in case an apothecary is not nearby. If all else fails, you have to make one from scratch."

"And what if that fails?" The professor asks, walking to the front of her desk and resting against it.

"Make them as comfortable as possible and make peace with the inevitable." Savannah's voice cracks, and I snap my attention toward her. There's a flash of sadness that washes over her features. But as soon as I blink, it's gone. Like it never existed in the first place.

I hate seeing my normally bubbly friend so affected by whatever is bothering her. We definitely need to catch up. Maybe she will share what's going on. Maybe we can help.

"Very good. You'll definitely save many lives."

Professor Crosswell smiles gently and moves to slowly pace in front of the class.

She stops and looks at another student behind us. "Yes, what is it?"

"What about the plague that's taking over the southern half of the country? What do you think about that? What about if it comes here?"

She pauses long enough to make me uncomfortable. "The magusari are working with healers and consultants to find a cure. We'll no doubt have one soon. Way before the plague reaches the island."

"We?" Milo asks. "Are you one of the consultants?"

The boys in the room begin murmuring, hungrily eyeing the professor. She smirks. "Now that we know what poisons and curses do, how to detect which was used, and how to reverse or cure said inflictions, what about protecting against either further attacks or even as prevention?"

Milo raises his hand.

The professor nods toward him. "Mr. Moreau?"

"Enchanted items designed specifically for the individual could help protect from curses and poisons on a generalized level. Wards are used as well. Sometimes in conjunction with alchemy, runes, and herbology. However, it's often best to just not piss anyone off."

The class bursts out in laughter. I chuckle too. It's true, though perfectly timed.

"That's no fun," Jesse says.

I shake my head. "Of course, you would have an issue with it."

"Duh."

Milo adds. "I'm looking forward to experimenting with new and innovative ways to extend protective wards."

I smile at him. "You never cease to amaze me, Milo."

He shoves his glasses further up his nose and shrugs, smiling bashfully.

The professor covers her mouth and turns her back to the room to hide her own laughter that bounces her shoulders. Once the humor of the talk dies down and the professor has fully recovered from the blunt yet hilarious truth, she faces the room once more.

"Within your textbooks, you will find a syllabus and list of assignments due at the next class. You're dismissed." Professor Crosswell stands at the head of the class and watches as each of us file out of the room. Her eyes rest on mine and she gives a short nod. I return the gesture. It's more of a curious look than anything, and with Jesse's responses to her questions, it's no wonder. She is probably curious as to what I see in him.

If only she knew.

I bump Savannah's shoulder with mine. She smiles at me. "So, when are we going to hang out?"

"What are you doing Saturday? We'll need a whole day to catch up." She winks.

I laugh. "I agree, and I have just the thing too."

"Spa day?" she asks.

"Sounds good to me," I say, acting like that wasn't what I was thinking. That's exactly what I need, and something tells me Savannah is long overdue for a day of being pampered. I'm excited and looking forward to it. It's been too long since we've been to Samish Island.

"I like your thinking." She nudges me with her elbow and laughs.

CHAPTER FIVE

The scenery that the secret training room has shifted to simply takes my breath away.

Gideon and I stand on a warm sunny beach of what I imagine is the mirror image of Blackbriar from before the academy was built. Neither a building nor tower constructed by human hands mars the lush, vivid landscape. It's truly a paradise, and one I hope to visit more often.

Next to the rushing blue waters of the Pacific Ocean as it rolls over the sand, smoothing the grains, Gideon stands behind me, hands resting just above my wrists as my eyes are closed and I listen to the way the island sings.

"Deep breaths," Gideon instructs, voice low and near my ears, his warm breath blowing over the skin on my neck, making it extremely difficult to keep my focus on the training instead of on my body's reaction.

I'm practicing water magic. After mastering fire and lightning, Gideon felt it suitable to learn how to master water next. Especially since I used it in the form of ice with the feral harpy eagle.

"Feel for the moisture in the air." Gideon's voice flows into my ear, sending chills down my neck and goosebumps poke out all over my arms.

I do as he says. The air is cold, strong, forceful. Nothing stops the wind. It flows regardless of what stands in its way. Flowing over the water, pushing the currents, over the mountain tops, between the trees in the forest, over the sand dunes. Within it, is the cooling force of water. Also an unstoppable force. Its power is strong, able to carry extremely heavy things, or churn damaging currents that rush invisible toward unsuspecting victims. It forms snow and feeds the land with rain.

Wind is beautiful. So is the icy moisture mixed in with it.

And the energy within it feels much like the way my magic does when Gideon is near me. Strong. Powerful.

I smile at that thought. Somehow, it's comforting

to know that if we are ever separated, the wind will always be there.

"Can you feel the force? The energy of the water?" Gideon asks.

I nod as my body quakes with need.

"Good. Pull that to you."

"How?" I ask.

He chuckles lightly in my ear. "Call to it with your magic."

Focusing, I reach into my magic and coax it to pull in the water. To surround us in a protective vortex. My mind wanders to how close Gideon is to me, his chest pressed to my back. His warmth seeping into my skin. With every inhale, he exhales warm breath along my skin, making my heart flutter and heat pool between my legs. His effect on my magic is much stronger today. But so is the effect of being so close to him.

I suck in a breath as the wind tugs toward me, sharpening my focus back to what I am supposed to be thinking about instead of dirty deeds between sheets. I call on the moisture within it, and I feel the icy trickle from before fill my veins. But something feels... off. The moment I snap back to the exercise versus my hormone-driven thoughts, the wind blows right into us, sending the both of us flying backward, landing on a small sand dune. Gideon grunts as I land on top of him, the full force of my weight slamming into his rock-hard abs, kicking the air from his lungs.

Quickly, I roll off of him and onto my knees, placing a hand on his chest as he coughs to catch his breath. "Oh crap. Are you okay?" My frantic question sounds a bit too shrill to my ears, but for some reason, Gideon laughs.

He freaking *laughs.*

"What the hell is so funny?" I ask, sitting up and propping my fists on my hips.

He doesn't stop as he rolls to his side and gets louder, laughing harder.

I move to my rump and pull my knees close to me, wrapping my arms around them. I'm rather offended that he's laughing at my almost being his demise. "Go ahead, I'll wait."

I peek at him from the corner of my eye as he finally makes it to his feet and stumbles toward me as though he's drunk. His bout of hysterics fades as he reaches out a hand toward me. "That was fun."

"I thought I hurt you!" I smack away his hand. But I can't stop the smile from tugging on my lips.

"I'm perfectly fine, Wren. Let's try again."

"Fine." I look him in his beautiful blue-green eyes. "But you may want to stand back this time."

"And miss out on another ride like that? Not a chance."

I laugh under my breath as I slap my hand into his and he pulls me up to my feet. "Your funeral."

"Doubtful." He spins me in his arms, sand grinding under my shoes as I once again have my back pressed against his firm chest, muscles rippling under his dress shirt. "This time, don't get distracted."

I roll my eyes as they squeeze shut and bite the corner of my lower lip. "Easy for you to say."

His breath pulses over my skin as he softly chuckles. His hands rest on my waist. I instinctively lean farther into him, bending my neck as I struggle to focus. "Watch."

That one word forces me to peel my eyes open from the blissful feeling of melting into him as I observe the wind flowing around us in a shield of water. In the vortex, everything is calm within a five-foot diameter. A wall of icy debris spins around us faster than anything I have seen before. Outside of the wall of cold water that spans the rest of the beach, the trees pull toward us bending with the force of the water being pulled from the air. The world around us is contorting with the unseen force of the tunnel we stand in the center of.

"Wow." It comes out as a whisper.

"It gets much easier with practice." Gideon releases my waist as he walks forward, and the tunnel follows. I quickly rush to him to keep up. He spins on his heels and faces me. There's a seriousness to his gaze. "Dismantle this."

I blankly stare at him. "How?"

"Call the water to you. Take the power from me. Tighten the circle a couple of feet."

I quirk an eyebrow, but with the hungry look in his eyes, I'm egged on. Still, I'm aware of all the ways this could go wrong. Either way, I know I'm safe with him. And that gives me the courage I need to try. "You make it sound so easy."

He chuckles. "Why don't you give it a shot?"

Closing my eyes, I reach for my magic and feel for the water. Suddenly, they are in tune with each other and I mentally tug on the water, using my magic to pull it closer to me. I feel Gideon getting closer and the toes of his shoes gently tap against mine. The tips of his fingers touch mine, and I release the water completely.

When I open my eyes, I'm ensnared by the most beautiful blue-green gaze smiling at me.

I jump up and throw my arms around Gideon. Excited that I have done it.

He wraps his arms around me and breathes in deep the scent of my hair. "Well done."

"You helped." I narrow my gaze on him, catching on to him cheating for me like that.

"You'll never be able to prove that." He squeezes me a little closer before loosening his arms. I take the hint and pull away. Not entirely, but enough. We still have to play things safe for now. Both of us know better than most we are a ticking time-bomb ready to explode at a moment's notice. I'm his trigger and gods know he's mine.

"You wouldn't," I say, narrowing my gaze on him and cocking my head just enough in what I hope would be a look to make him weak in the knees and tell me everything I want to know.

Instead, he smiles and brushes my hair from over my shoulder. "Guess you'll have to figure that out."

"Not fair." I playfully smack his upper arm.

His hands slide along my waist, pulling me gently closer to him as his eyes focus on my mouth. Just as tenderly, his mouth presses against mine. Gingerly, he kisses me, almost like he's afraid to break me, and that causes a small sense of panic inside me. But soon enough, the kiss deepens and becomes more heated and passionate. The panic ebbs and fades into need.

He moves one hand to the small of my back as his

other moves to the back of my head, tangling his fingers in my hair as I grip the back of his shirt in my fists.

I don't want this to stop. I want him to give in finally, to finish what he's started so many times before. Always pushing the cusp just a little bit closer to the edge of my self-control.

And just like always, before I reach my breaking point, he pulls away, panting for breath. He rests his forehead against mine and I grip his wrist to keep him from letting go of me.

"I'm sorry," he whispers. "I shouldn't have."

"Stop apologizing." I nudge him gently with my nose, giving him permission to take more of what we both obviously want.

He shakes his head, pulling me to his chest and holding me. "We just have to wait two more years to explore our growing affection for each other."

"You're honorable to a fault. You know that?" I tightly cling to him, listening to him breathe and forcing the quaking desire to ease.

"Even still, what I've allowed to progress has been more than I should have, but I can't help the way I'm drawn to you. I can't get enough. Every moment you're not in my presence feels like hours."

I smile as my heart fills with immense joy. "Two more years?"

He huffs a sigh. "We can do this. I'm not going anywhere. I promise." He kisses the top of my head and it melts me just a little more.

"Are you sure we won't implode before then?" I ask.

He chuckles as he pulls away from me, keeping a hold of my hand. "Dear gods, I hope not." He shrugs. "We should have enough to keep us occupied until then. You with your studies, and me with my headmaster duties. Our team with the Order and their movements."

"Speaking of," I say as we begin to walk toward the door materializing as the world around us shifts back into the closet, "any word?"

"No. Unfortunately. They're unusually quiet."

"Why does that sound worse than knowing?" I ask as we step through the closet and into Gideon's office.

"It unsettles me as well. They are up to something likely big and unexpected."

"I guess we'll just have to keep our guards up and eyes open."

He nods as he takes a seat at his desk. "Indeed. So, Soren told me about the attack with the harpy eagle."

"Yeah that was fun." It comes out just as sarcastically as I wanted it to.

He gives me a look that tells me he wants more detail. And I tell him. Everything that I could recall from the encounter. He nods and takes in all the information. Once I'm done, he sighs. "It's a good thing you weren't hurt any worse than you were. Next time we are able to, I'll help you practice the ice. Sounds like your magic is naturally evolving, coming to you when you need it most. Quite fascinating."

I chuckle. "I'm glad you think so."

He checks his watch. "Our time is up, I'm afraid."

I nod and stand from the desk, meeting him halfway as he walks around to give me a quick hug and kiss. We smile one last time at each other and I turn for the door. Just before I leave, I'm reminded of Milo's penchant for experiments in his room, and Gideon's promise to get him a room dedicated for those.

I spin around. "Oh, don't forget about that room for Milo's experiments. It should probably be fireproof."

Gideon's wide-eyed look and lips forming a slight "O" takes the cake. I wink and walk out of the room.

My job here is done.

CHAPTER SIX

For the umpteenth time tonight, I'm startled awake with either the sensation of being watched or horrible visions.

It's obscenely late, and with classes in the morning, I desperately need sleep. But not just any sleep. Good sleep. However, rest evades me as images flood my mind of my traitorous aunt and her cold last words to me as she tried to strike me down. I could have lost everything that night. My men fought by my side, and I was able to recover my father.

Still, that bloody battle haunts me.

What kind of person would choose the Order over her own family? What power, privilege, or hold did they sway Aunt Patricia with? She had told me they were her new family. But in embracing the Order, she nearly destroyed her own flesh and blood. Perhaps my lack of sleep is due to my brain trying to process all this. My own messed up way to let go of any latent guilt or regret. I would've helped Aunt Patricia if she had asked—if she truly wanted to change.

But it's too late now. And I'm left wondering if it all could've turned out differently.

As the minutes continue to tick by, I'm increasingly aware of how much less functional I'm going to be in the morning. Had I still been with the trolls, lack of sleep would be a different story. I was accustomed to little or no shut-eye. Constantly on alert, snapping my attention toward each and every creak and crunch that surrounded me. Because those noises were usually followed by a vicious troll looking to send me on a dangerous errand or beat me for the hell of it.

But now? Now, I have grown accustomed to sleeping hours uninterrupted, and I freaking love that.

Tonight, however, I close my eyes and see things like Anderson's face, all scrunched up in anger, trying to steal every last ounce of my energy until my mind is broken like Jesse's poor mother. The image of my aunt, hovering over my father as she drains the life from him, and me being powerless to stop it. Images of me being held captive by the Order as they strap me to a strange machine with a large needle aimed at my abdomen, painfully pulling my meteorite out of me.

Okay, so it's restless sleep. But still. If I don't get some rest soon, I'll be utterly useless tomorrow.

The feeling that surrounds me in the room evokes the sickening sensation Anderson had given me when he thought he was being sneaky, stealing my energy like I was a god damn buffet. Though I'd like to think he wouldn't come back, not now, and certainly not to Blackbriar, the feeling is so potent that he might as well be standing in the corner, silently waiting with that smug smirk on his face, just waiting for the moment to pounce and have all that he can take of me and probably more. And that unsettles me to no end. It's such a profound feeling, and I hadn't felt anything like it since then.

Until now.

It makes me question when a zacar steals someone's energy, if even the tiniest piece of his own is shared in the unfair exchange, allowing these uncomfortable sensations to bleed through at the most inopportune moments. Or, if this is something else.

I have been pushing myself hard, trying to keep up with classes and staying on top of my game. I'm not sure where this feeling is coming from or what's evoking it. But searching through my room, in all the darkened corners and shadows, I'm still alone. All is as it should be.

Well, Anderson isn't here. And should he ever show his face again, he'll be sorry. Because not only will I finish what he started, but I'll end it *forever*.

I sit up in my bed, now in disarray with my blankets and sheets tangled into a mess, and let out a long, exasperated breath. When I lived with the trolls, the only thing that would help tire me out was taking a nice, long walk.

But the energy needed to pull myself out of bed is far out of reach, and I see that I have a choice to make. Force myself to get out of bed, take that walk that I know will help, or settle in for the rest of this long, restless night and be a zombie in the morning.

I fall back onto my pillow as the feeling of being watched becomes overwhelming. It's too prominent. Too palpable. Too unnerving.

With a huff, I jump up from my bed and turn on every single light to inspect my room. Maybe for the third time. I can't recall. Every time it's the same thing throughout this seemingly endless night. Nothing to be seen. But this time, I groggily search for an illusion. Even now, the lights bleed into every inch of my room, shoving the shadows away. My window is still closed, the curtains drawn, the fireplace cold, my bathroom is empty, nothing in my room stands out as out of place. Everything is in its rightful place.

I don't get it, and I'm growing more frustrated with the lack of sleep to the point that I decide to go for that walk. I'm up anyway. What harm could it do?

Sliding on my leather jacket and slippers, I head out the door and toward my favorite, most peaceful and serene spot ever.

The gardens.

The halls of the castle are eerily quiet, and that sense of being watched, the weight of unseen eyes resting on my shoulders, doesn't let up. I briefly entertain the idea of sneaking into Milo or Jesse's bed for the rest of the night, but I would hate to disturb them. They probably wouldn't mind, but with it being so late, I would rather handle this on my own.

I keep checking my surroundings as I continue to move toward the gardens, wanting to see if I can catch the creepy observer in the act, but I'm alone, except for some of the statues that stand guard in the halls.

Passing by Gideon's office, I pause and notice that the painting is of a calm, blissful evening. It makes me frown, because I feel anything but calm.

As soon as my feet touch the familiar stone of the path into the main garden, I already feel better. My skin cools, comforted by the late night summer island breeze. The sky is clear, showing off the dazzling diamonds glittering in the navy-blue sky. The moon is turning yellow as it sets along the horizon, and I realize that it is much later than I gave the hour credit for.

But that feeling of being watched, thankfully, has ebbed. I wonder what that was about. What does it mean? Am I working myself too hard?

Regardless, that's what this walk is for. To think, to clear my mind, to relax and get tired enough that no matter what disturbance lies in the air, I'm able to sleep.

I let out a soft sigh as I try to force back the frustration that fact brings me. I rub out my shoulders as I walk and make my way toward the edge of the garden that overlooks the ocean. The view reminds me of the one back in Idaho. The way the lake reflected the night sky and gave me hope of better things to come. That seems like a lifetime ago. A distant dream come true.

Because my life has gotten much better, and it's improving by the day. Sure, I have some obstacles to overcome, but who doesn't? With my men—my family —by my side, I can do anything.

"Well good evening, Miss Blackwood," a familiar woman's voice says.

I turn toward the academy's Patron Mage and smile. "Good evening, Lady Alene."

"Troubles sleeping?" she asks as she approaches me. As soon as we are side by side, she walks with me.

"That's one way to phrase it," I mutter.

She nods and thoughtfully pauses before speaking. "Would you like to share with me the issue you are having?"

"I keep fighting the sense of being watched. It's almost like there's something horribly wrong, and I can't place my finger on it. Plus, when I do manage to get a shred of sleep, it's filled with nightmares. Like they're twisted versions of things in my past." I shudder.

As I spill my proverbial guts to Lady Alene, she takes it all in with nods of understanding and not an ounce of judgement. I love that about her.

"Do you want to be more specific? Perhaps I can help you find meaning in it all and ease your worries?"

I shrug. "The biggest one is about Anderson."

"I see." Her voice comes off gentle and soothing. Like a mother calming a child from a bad dream. I wonder if this is what my own mother had done for me. She died so long ago, I barely remember her.

"I don't know, it was... different than what Anderson did to me. But the sensation is so much the same." I shake my head and pinch the bridge of my nose. After sucking in a deep breath, I let it out through my pursed lips. "The meteorite within me—my magic—has given me warnings or urgings in the past. I don't know if it's trying to tell me something, or just a little screwed up after everything that's happened. It's all sudden and doesn't make sense."

"Is that the only thing keeping you awake?"

I shake my head. "There's one where I don't make it to my father in time and my aunt kills him, and one where the Order actually succeeds in capturing me to steal my powers."

She nods. "I can understand why sleep is difficult tonight. If I may suggest a few tips?"

"Please." We slow our steps and halt. I face her as she takes my hands into her cold stone ones. A bright blue light bursts between our hands, and when it's over, something rests between them, laying on my palm with cool, calming rivers of peace working its way through me.

Lady Alene moves her hands and I see a small charm, metallic, mostly, but littered throughout it are small light-purple and pink stones surrounded by a shimmering design that is a mix of curls.

Ivy. That's what it reminds me of. Little strands of ivy with the stones acting like flowers.

"Keep this with you. It will help you find peace."

"It's already working," I say, amazed at the rush of peaceful calm flooding me from head to toe. "Thank you so much, Lady."

She nods. "It is my pleasure. Anything I can do to help is my honor."

I smile.

"It may surprise you, but when I was feeling particularly restless, I would do something similar to what we are doing now."

"You had difficulties sleeping?" I ask.

Not her. Not the kickass Patron Mage whose exploits I've read about.

She softly chuckles. "Yes, even I had my fair share of normal problems." She sighs as she looks at the stars. "That was such a long time ago. Obviously, I don't need sleep any longer."

I stifle a giggle. "No, I suppose not."

"Feeling better?"

I nod, smiling. My shoulders are relaxed, and my body feels lighter somehow. Almost like I'm floating or gliding over the ground instead of stepping on it.

"Good. Now, off to bed."

"Yes, ma'am," I say with a smile.

She softly laughs. "Shall I walk with you?"

"I would love that."

Most of the trek toward the castle is quiet and peaceful. I'm not sure if it's the company I'm with or the charm, or even both. But I'm loving it. I take note of the frost coating the leaves of the trees and bushes we pass, and everything glitters with delight and wonder.

Man, I love my life.

We reach the back entrance to the academy and Lady Alene turns to face me. "Even in the darkest of times, there is a light inside you. Look toward that light, and all will work out just fine."

I nod. "I appreciate the words of wisdom. I'll carry them with me."

"Goodnight, my friend."

"Goodnight, Lady."

By the time I reach my bed again, the room feels different. Softer. Quieter. I don't feel like I'm being watched anymore. I'm secure. No sooner than my body lays down and I cover myself up to my nose with my blanket do I fall asleep.

CHAPTER SEVEN

I never thought I would say this in my entire life, but... I hate the sun right now.

It's too bright. Too cheery. Too all the things I don't have the energy to deal with right now. Despite getting a few hours of solid, restful sleep, I'm exhausted. And judging by the look of it, so is Milo.

However, our desire for sleep hasn't prevented us from hanging out with Jesse and Savannah. We trekked to a hard to reach, private shore on Blackbriar that Savannah got permission for us to spend the evening at. It's even complete with a fire pit. It's a special occasion type place only.

The rocky island cove that we are sitting in provides just the right backdrop to make it feel like we are on vacation on some remote island in the middle of the ocean. I even entertain the idea that we are the first settlers here.

It helps to pass the time. Don't judge me.

Jesse and Savannah have way too much energy as they try to coax Milo and I into their antics.

"Swimming is good for the soul!" Savannah says.

"It'll probably help wake you up," Jesse adds.

"Or make me even more exhausted," I mutter.

"I'm not much of a swimmer even if I had sleep." Milo is barely keeping his eyes open. He's awfully pale. I frown.

Jesse shakes his head. "You both need to slow down and take your time. Seriously, learn to pace your workaholic selves better. Honestly, Wren, haven't I taught you anything?"

I glare at him. "Not funny."

He quirks an eyebrow. "Of course, I am, but I'll forgive you this once. Exhaustion and all."

"I don't know, Jesse," Savannah says, walking up to me and Milo and squatting in front of us. She gently examines our faces. "I think this is more than just lack of sleep."

"I hope not." I lay my head on Milo's shoulder. "Otherwise, my plan of just getting more sleep is going to have less than great results."

She shrugs. "Sleep, and maybe a nice soothing tea

mixed with valerian root, may just be the thing you need. Having nightmares?" She switches her gaze between me and Milo.

"I just didn't sleep well. Feel drained," Milo answers.

She nods with a slight frown and looks at me. I sigh. "Sort of."

"Hmm…" She stands and faces Jesse. "I think we need to take these two to the infirmary."

I look at Jesse as he stands there with a deep frown. But I can tell he's not upset at Milo and me for ruining the fun, just that he's bothered with how miserable we both look. Whatever Savannah figured out, Jesse has too. Whatever it is, it's not good.

Oh joy.

"Come on you two," Jesse says. "Off to the infirmary we go."

He pulls me up by the arm and Savannah takes the brunt of my weight, supporting me with an arm around my waist.

"I'm fine," I say, trying to pull away and not having enough strength to wiggle free from Savannah's grip.

"Yeah…" Savannah says, studying the way I wobble a little on my feet. "You're going."

"No. Really. I'm fine. Just need a good night's rest." I admit I'm a bit out of character, and I appreciate their concern. But I know I'll feel better after tonight.

"I would feel better if you went," Jesse adds, a concerned expression on his face almost makes me give in. Almost.

I glare at him. "No. I'm fine. I promise. If the sleep doesn't help, then I'll get checked out. I got this. Truly. I appreciate your concern though."

"I'll also go on Monday if I'm not better over the weekend," Milo says. He stifles a yawn. "Gonna spend it all in bed."

His eyes slip a little out of focus, and I wonder if he's going to fall over and start snoring in the next few seconds.

"Now, I know something is wrong with him," Jesse says. "Since when do you prefer to stay in bed and throw out all that precious time on your experiments, hmm?"

"Since I'm exhausted and can barely keep my eyes open," he mutters.

Savannah props her hands on her hips. "Honestly, you two."

"Stubborn is as stubborn does," Jesse says as he walks to the fire pit and kicks around the charred logs from its previous use. "Think I need to get some wood? Maybe a nice fire will help them snap out of this."

"No," Savannah says, "I think we'll have to wait until next time for camping out. I think these two need their own beds."

I nod, agreeing with that statement, and lean into Milo a little more. His shoulder is so comfortable. Milo's head droops onto mine and he sighs blissfully. I smile, snuggling into him. I could probably just nap here and wake up feeling great in an hour or so.

"Speaking of," Savannah adds, "we should cancel our spa date for tomorrow."

"No." I level my gaze on her. Milo groans as he has to lift his head from mine.

"I think it would be best." Her insistence is not helping. Honestly, it's just a lack of sleep. I knew I was going to be rather sluggish today. It's not that big of a deal.

Probably.

"I don't," I argue. "We need it. We're going. I'm not accepting no for an answer."

"Fine. As long as you promise to be checked out first if you still feel like this." Savannah sits in front of me and leans back on the sand. She studies me for a moment, and I feel like she's trying to detect a hint of a lie or whatever is going on with me so she can return to her argument of going to the infirmary.

"Knew you'd see it my way." I smile sleepily.

"There's a little bit of the Wren we all know and love," Jesse says as he takes a seat on the other side of me.

"I aim to please," I say as my lips stretch wide.

That seems to take the worry off me. For the moment at least. But now, both Jesse and Savannah are eyeing Milo, waiting for him to prove he's really okay. That it is just coincidence we both feel like utter crap today.

"What?" he asks as he sits a little straighter.

Savannah shakes her head as she smiles while Jesse stands there with a quirked eyebrow.

"Come on, man. Do something only you would do," Jesse says.

Milo groans, rolling his eyes. He settles himself against the rocky cave wall and looks above us. He lazily points to the ceiling. "This used to be submerged in water."

Savannah, Jesse, and I all look up and the jagged edges of the ceiling are cast in shadow from the slowly setting sun.

"How can you tell?" I ask, completely curious. It's a

sensation I wasn't expecting to experience amid all this exhaustion.

Milo yawns and seems to struggle to open his eyes. "The water marks on the stone." He sounds almost drunk as the words slur together.

I narrow my eyes, trying to focus on the lines on the wall. There are some darker lines, I wonder if that's what he's referring to? I don't want to ask as it seems to take a lot of effort for him to explain, and I know he doesn't have the energy for it. Still, it's good enough for me.

Settling my gaze on Savannah and Jesse, they stare at the cave walls, deciphering Milo's point.

"Satisfied yet?" I ask.

Savannah shrugs. "Good enough for me."

"I don't know," Jesse says, "I think he has more compelling points in him."

I frown at him. "Don't push your luck."

"Well you're no fun," he remarks and smiles.

I shake my head. That's my Jesse all right.

As we settle into our discussion, becoming more playful, it's calm and relaxing, just the four of us chilling, hanging out and enjoying each other's company to the best of our current ability. But the one thing I can't shake is the feeling from last night. I know there is more behind it, but I'm too damned tired to try and figure it out. But I know it's going to bug me until I do.

"Quiet one," Jesse says, "up for a game of charades?"

I shrug. I could probably go for a nice diversion right now. Anything to get my mind off of last night. "Milo?"

"Anything to pass the time and get to bed faster, but I have a feeling this isn't going to be traditional charades."

"You know me so well," Jesse says placing a hand on his heart. "I knew he loved me." He bats his eyes as Savannah laughs at him. I barely manage a chuckle. But his shenanigans are working.

"What's the version we are playing?" I ask.

Jesse fist pumps the air and hops up from the sandy ground. He stands near the fire pit. "The point of the game is... well, I don't have a name for it." He shrugs. "But it's fun. So, I'm going to create an illusion, and your job is to figure out what is real, and what is not..."

I snort. "Sounds like a boring game."

"*Au contraire*, my dear. It's quite difficult. Observe."

As he explains, Savannah takes Jesse's spot.

"Don't get comfortable there, missy." Jesse points at the spot Savannah took. "That spot is mine."

She shrugs. "I stole it fair and square."

I can barely focus on the demonstration. All I can see is multiples of Jesse performing tricks. "I don't get it."

"Which one of us is the real one?" all of the Jesses ask, and it almost makes my head spin.

"This is giving me a headache," I mutter, eyes blurring from focusing too much on trying to point out the real Jesse.

All of the Jesses frown. "That's not being a good sport, now is it?"

"Maybe we should just hang out and relax?" Savannah offers.

"Fine." The Jesses bleed and blend together until only one remains. The real one. "Party poopers."

"Maybe next time?" Milo says as he rests his head against my shoulder.

We spend the rest of the evening with me and Milo struggling for some semblance of human normalcy, rapidly running out of steam to keep going, while Jesse and Savannah are the more coherent ones, chatting idly and trying to keep me and Milo in the conversation as much as possible. As the sun starts to lower beyond the watery horizon, I give up. "I need to go to bed."

With a sigh and a groan, we head back.

Jesse helps keep Milo on his feet and Savannah

helps me. The trek is especially difficult on the way back. It's a hard to reach place on the island, but it's also hard to get back. And now that I'm even more exhausted, I'm relying more on Savannah's help than I feel great about.

My thoughts become wrapped around Milo and how he's doing. He's much paler than normal, and it looks like he's running on fumes. It's not like him to be like this. It also doesn't escape my notice that though we have similar ailments today, his is by far the worst. I almost wonder if someone slipped something into our food or something. Maybe we drank from the wrong fountain?

Either way, while Savannah and Jesse seem to have enough energy for the four of us, Milo and I don't.

We decide to take a different path back, a short cut, according to Jesse. Once we arrive at a rope bridge, I'm reminded of my trial where I had to bring it across the gorge just so I could cross it before whatever was in the woods caught me.

As the sky darkens into night even more, I'm well aware that though this may be a shortcut, it's a bad one.

"Jesse, we can't be here after dark." Warning is thick in my voice. Savannah pulls me tighter against her. We're not supposed to talk about our trials, but it seems that, judging by the seriousness in her expression, she knows about these woods as well.

"I got an illusion covering us," he says, like he's deep in thought. It must be taking a lot out of him to keep an illusion going and carrying most of Milo's weight. "Let's take a break."

"As long as it's quick," Milo mutters, slumping to the ground against a large boulder near the left side of the bridge.

"Relax, I've got us covered," Jesse says as he takes a seat on the boulder.

Savannah releases me, and I sit at the base of a tree. She can't seem to let herself relax though. She keeps her attention spread over our surroundings, carefully watching for every little movement.

That confirms she had gone through either something similar or worse than I did during the trials.

I feel myself slipping in and out of consciousness for the ten to fifteen minutes we break. Jesse claps his hands loudly, startling me. "Let's continue, then."

Carefully, Jesse and Milo cross the bridge first. Savannah and I cross next. From here, it will be a relatively easy way back. The groves aren't that far up ahead, and soon enough, we will reach the castle, and our blissful beds.

After a few more breaks, we make it back.

Savannah walks me to my room and I collapse onto my bed. "Thanks for the help back," I mutter, half asleep.

"My pleasure. Sleep well, my friend." Her footsteps whisper through the room and out the door that closes with a soft click.

I don't bother taking off my clothes much less my shoes. I just flip off the light and curl into my soft pillow, breathing in the scent of my comforter.

Before long, my eyes drift closed, and I'm carried off to blissful, deep sleep.

CHAPTER EIGHT

The sunshine is a welcome sight as I peel my eyes open after finally sleeping well.

For once, my night wasn't riddled with nightmares and I was able to sleep uninterrupted with ease. I think I had exhausted myself, needed the recharge.

With a satisfied grin, I brush a finger against the ivy leaf charm Lady Alene had given me, grateful for her assistance. I threaded a chain through it and am wearing it around my neck. The enchantment worked so well that I feel as if the night before never happened. But I know it's only a temporary fix, and whatever is plaguing me, I'll have to eventually deal with it head-on.

But first, my long-awaited spa day with my good friend, Savannah.

I quickly jump up and get dressed, throwing on comfortable and warm clothing. I stop in the bathroom to run a brush through my hair, tying it back into a messy bun, and brush my teeth before I grab my leather jacket and rush out of House of Phoenix's common room. I'm appreciative of the solitude of the halls on an early Saturday morning. It's peaceful, and I can move freely through the halls without being hindered by large crowds. My belly grumbles with its need to be fed, so I make a quick detour for the kitchens. My mouth waters as the scent of fresh baked pastries fills my nostrils, and I spot one of the cooks, Caseus, placing a large basket of muffins and Danishes at a self-serve counter.

"You're up early," he says as he turns toward me. He pauses and falters, as if he'd been expecting someone else. "I wasn't expecting anyone to come in for another hour."

My lips press into a thin line. Was there some rule that I couldn't have an early snack? "I just wanted to grab one of these on my way out, actually." I point toward a very inviting chocolate chip muffin.

He grins, but it's the kind where you know the person doing it doesn't really like you. I quirk an eyebrow but put on my best fake smile in return. He uses a set of tongs to pick up the pastry and sets it on a small plate for me. "I... also have a recent batch of black tea, with fresh milk and spices. It's in the back, I'll fetch you a cup."

His matter-of-fact tone rubs me the wrong way.

"I don't want to be late. I'm meeting a friend, but thanks."

I swipe my muffin from the plate and give him an awkward wave before rushing out of the castle and to the dock at the northern end of the island to meet Savannah. The air is chilly, and a thin layer of frost covers the ground in the more shaded areas where the sun has yet to reach.

I pull my leather jacket closer around me as I walk down the stairs toward the creaky dock. I can already hear the old captain's mutterings as I move closer. The breeze lifts wisps of his shaggy grey hair, and he pauses to adjust his double-breasted vest. Looks like the brass buttons on his vest are newly polished. I'll give him credit for sprucing himself up a bit, even seems like he ran a comb through his beard, though he's still rambling about striking down snakes. I shake my head. He's quite the character, that one. At least the trip will have free entertainment.

I spot Savannah on the vessel that still looks like a rickety old sailing boat with seats along the back and side, as I step onto the dock. She smiles and waves. I pick up my pace, waving back. Once I'm carefully on the boat, I plop into my seat next to her and smile in greeting.

"Feeling better?" She asks, her amethyst eyes taking in my face. "You look like you are."

"Definitely feeling better. Glad we didn't reschedule?"

She nods. "You look very rested."

I chuckle. "You look as gorgeous as ever."

"Thank you." She poses like a model, which makes me only laugh harder. "Did you run into Milo on the way here?"

"Nope." I frown. He looked worse for wear yesterday, and I wasn't sure he would make it through the weekend without having to go to the infirmary. "You?"

She smiles and slowly bobs her head. "I have. He's doing quite well. Checked on him before I left." She winks knowingly at me.

I sigh in relief, sinking into my seat a little more. Seeing Milo the way he looked yesterday bothers me. I hated that he felt the way he did all day long. It seemed whatever he experienced was far worse than what I felt. I'm glad he's feeling better.

"I saw him on the way to his lab. At least, I hope that's where he was going with all the supplies he was carrying."

Good. Gideon kept his word about providing Milo a private room to work on his side projects. That's one less worry, at least. Now Milo can safely perform his experiments without burning down his bedroom.

"I bet he had a cheesy smile on his face too." I smile, picturing his sexy, nerdy grin as though he's standing in front of me right now.

"He was actually muttering to himself," she says and settles her gaze on me. Her eyebrows pull toward each other. "I think it was some sort of experiment he was trying to memorize." She shrugs. "He was in good spirits when I stopped him and checked in on him."

"Good. Sounds like he's back to himself as well. I wonder if it was something we ate?"

"It's possible. I mean, no one else got the same symptoms. But that doesn't necessarily mean there wasn't anything wrong with the food. *Blech*. Did you have the chicken parmigiana?"

The boat's motor roars to life and the vessel jerks forward as the captain heads us in the direction of Samish Island. Sea spray hits us in the face. It's like a thousand tiny needles stinging my skin. Thinking about it, we probably could have taken a portal there. But this is tradition.

What was that saying about hindsight?

Yeah, that.

Either way, the salty spray doesn't stop Savannah and me from catching up. It's a small annoyance at best, and this makes the trip feel more natural and normal.

"So, tell me about your summer," I say.

She shrugs, and that ever-permanent smile falters. At the sight of it, my heart sinks a little, and a part of me feels guilty for bringing up a sensitive matter. But it confirms that my intuition was correct. Something *is* wrong.

"It was a very rough summer." Her voice is lackluster, and I wish I hadn't asked just to have my bubbly friend back. This is supposed to be a time to relax and unwind, to escape the stresses of school and dealing with the machinations of the Order.

"Do you want to talk about it?" At least it's up to her now to continue the conversation. I let her know I'm here, now the ball is in her court.

"It's the plague. The disease that no one can figure out has spread throughout the southern states. So many lives lost. Human communities are even more in the dark, thinking it's some super virus or something."

"That's horrible."

"My dad and brothers are around it all the time. They wear special masks and gloves while helping their patients. But what's worse is they've quarantined themselves from the rest of the family as a precaution. It makes me so mad to think that he's preparing for the possibility of contracting the disease, knowing we don't have a cure yet. My dad's been working day and night on this, and the only thing he's established is that it's an airborne disease. It infects people who breathe it in."

I groan. That's even worse. An airborne disease like that might as well be a bio-weapon. The Order really is aiming to do damage. Deep down, my gut tells me they're guiding this. No wonder students at Blackbriar are worried about it reaching our island.

"I'm so sorry," I say, but the words feel cheap. "Is there anything we can do to help out?"

She shakes her head. "My dad won't allow it. He wants me to stay as far away as possible until they can figure out how to contain and defeat it. He's already informed the council and asked for help in preventing the spread as much as possible. They're even recruiting retired healers and experts to help reverse-engineer samples for a cure. For now, it's just a wait and see what happens."

"I'm sure your dad and everyone working on this will find a cure soon. It must be hard to know he's in the middle of all this."

She shrugs a shoulder. "It is, but I can keep myself occupied easily enough. Like with a spa day."

Just like that, her smile is back.

But I can tell she's trying hard to cheer me up, when it should be the other way around.

I return the gesture, though it feels half-hearted, and pull out the gift-certificate from my birthday last year. "Got you covered."

She grins. "You're supposed to use those on yourself."

"Where's the fun in that?" I ask.

"How was your summer?" She asks, changing the subject.

"It was good. You know, same ol', same ol'. Went to Crimson Isles, fought off a feral harpy eagle with Soren, had to file a report about it with a magusari captain, visited my dad, training... "

Her eyes widen. "A harpy eagle attacked you?"

We both jerk and slide across the built-in bench as the captain makes a sharp turn. He glances at us over his shoulder. Satisfied that we haven't flown out of the boat and drowned, he returns to steering us toward Samish Island.

After staring daggers at the old man's back, I face Savannah. "It was an eaglet, and Soren believes it was feral. They're running tests on the remains to see if they can uncover anything else."

She nods. "Good. It's almost unheard of for harpy eagles to roam free. They're heavily controlled."

"Gods help me." The captain chuckles, his back still turned to us. "Heavily controlled. And if that's the case, who *controlled* it to land on Crimson Isles? It's those snakes!"

I swear this guy needs a vacation. Maybe I'll get an extra spa certificate so he can get a massage and haircut.

Soon we arrive on the dock and make our way toward the spa with my gift certificates from my birthday in the back pocket of my jeans. My leather jacket crinkles as I move and shift, and the smile on my face at what is to come is nearly permanent.

Samish Island has a lot of small-town charm for such a populated area. Giant evergreens stab at the sky, towering above the old clocktower at the center of town. A road curves around it, leading farther into town to homes and even a grocery center. Somewhere, here in the city's center, is a shop of magical goods and supplies that keeps Blackbriar stocked. I haven't been there though. I prefer to visit Crimson Isles for all my needs. Gives me an excuse to visit my dad.

The buildings are reminiscent of Cape Cod style

structures and are stacked close together, leaving little room between each. Smack dab in the middle of it all, is the spa.

As we step through the door, I inhale a deep breath of lavender and rosemary.

Once we are led to our room where the pampering will be exquisite, we settle into our lounges and are handed mimosas. I glance at Savannah as her smile fades and a shadow crosses her eyes.

"You okay?" I ask.

She nods and sets her mimosa on the small black table next to her. "Yeah. I am."

"Worried about your dad and brothers?"

She nods and presses her lips together. I can tell she's trying not to cry.

I hate to see her this way. Not my cheerful Savannah who more than once lifted me up when I felt down. I wish there was something I could say to make her smile or laugh. But, sometimes, silence is all right. Sometimes it's just nice to know someone is there with you and you're not alone.

I down my mimosa a little too quickly and reach for her hand, giving it a firm squeeze. After all we've been through, we'll get through this too. As a team. As friends.

CHAPTER NINE

The halls are strewn with white iridescent ribbons in celebration of our Patron Mage, Lady Alene. Tapestries with the image of her mortal face hang in every single hallway. The painting that changes and moves in front of Gideon's office shows her standing in the garden in her human form, holding a flower to her nose. Regal and beautiful. This is a celebration visited once every one-hundred years. I'm excited that we are doing a special ceremony for Lady Alene. She's been such a wonderful support for me, and I feel like I can return the favor and show my gratitude with this celebration.

As I make my way to the arena, I notice some of the students taking the festivities seriously by dressing up in ancient garb, reminiscent of Lady Alene's time, complete with the blond hair forming ringlets over their shoulders. There are even members of the council here. I only know this by their sashes listing their positions. High councilman, low councilman, chancellor, viceroy, count... the list is endless, and a bit daunting to be among such high ranks. The dignitaries of the mage community.

This celebration is quite the big deal.

I quirk an eyebrow as a few more pass me by. One looks at me curiously as he passes by me. I don't know who he is or what his name is, but he seems friendly as he smiles and nods. Shaking my head, I force down the urge to laugh. Our Patron Mage is well loved here. This day is all about her. Her favorite foods are being prepared in the kitchens, her favorite pastimes are being enjoyed in the fields. Everything.

As I get closer to the arena, there are easels set up in the hall with paintings that come to life and show various events of her life. One shows a dangerous battle between Lady Alene and what seems to be a shadow mage. The lady holds lightning in her right hand, preparing to strike down the opposing mage who is attempting to take her out with shadowy, snake-like ropes shooting out from his fingers. Just before the smoky tentacles can reach her, she strikes the mage with lightning, causing him to falter in his attack. She leaves no time for him to react as she uses her left hand to freeze him into a solid form of ice.

I stare in awe and wonder. Not only is Lady Alene the most gentle spirit anyone could possibly have on their side, but she was a fierce badass in her time. It's an honor to count her as a friend.

Another image stands a few feet away. I quickly approach it to see what other magnificent accomplishments the Lady made during her mortal life.

In this one, she fights with another mage at her side. He's handsome and young, seemingly about my age. Together they face off a large group of shadow mages. Lady Alene conjures up vines from the ground, beneath the feet of the shadow mages, wrapping them in a cocoon of thick green rope. Her counterpart uses wind to disorient the others. But it's not without a challenge.

The shadow mages cheat.

A small group of five approaches from behind.

I hold my breath as it seems like the Lady and her companion aren't aware of them. Inch by inch, they draw closer, dark magic filling their hands as they move through the shadows, closing the gap between them and the Lady and her companion.

Together, the Lady and her companion join arms. He supports her as she lifts her feet, and he spins her, taking them out with powerful kicks. It's a move so fluid and smooth that the shadow mages didn't even see her coming.

"Yes!" my voice echoes above the fray of excited chatter. A few students look at me with curious expressions, some of them with concern. I shrug.

Further down the hallway is an image of Lady Alene's statue glowing softly with an array of colors, pulsing in and out, encircling her while ash, smoke, destroyed bodies, and crumbled walls surround her.

This must be when she became Blackbriar's Patron Mage. The sight evokes a sense of loss, love, and of the ultimate sacrifice.

I pull myself away and move on.

Even the doors to the arena are magically morphed into a wrought iron gate. Inside, the room is changed into the garden that she lives in for much of the time, brimming with blooming flowers, the smell of fresh green grass, flowering hedges, and large budding trees with beautiful lanterns that glow with the light of small moons.

The garden is decorated with white iridescent ribbons dangling from the trees and wrapped around the hedges. Some even dangle from the tops of lamp posts. It feels like they're really bringing the outside in. Considering a fresh layer of snow covers the ground outside, it's no wonder why. The arena looks like it's springtime, versus winter.

As soon as I step through, I'm formally announced magically by a floating megaphone painted brass with white iridescent ribbons hanging from it. How fun is that? It's like stepping into the past and seeing what life could have been like when Lady Alene was alive. Very regal. I sigh and try not to let the burning filling my cheeks stand out too much. I'll never live that down. Especially if Jesse sees me.

Speaking of... As I settle my gaze to the left, I find him. He smiles and waves me over, and I see that he is standing with Savannah. My steps falter as I notice Milo isn't around. It's not like him to be missing, especially on a day like this that happens literally once a century. I wonder if he's sick again.

Maybe I should go check.

First, I'll find out if Savannah or Jesse has seen him yet.

"There she is!" Jesse says, drinking in my length. "Not a very festive attire, but damn, those curves." He slides his hands along my waist and lets out a delicious moan that sends delightful tingles through me.

I chuckle. "Hello to you, too." I wink and playfully pull away. He hams up a humorous reaction as if I caused him significant pain as he bends his fingers against my skin. Almost like he supposedly hurt himself by touching me.

"What took you so long to get here?" Savannah asks.

I shrug. "I had to change out of the uniform."

She shakes her head while laughing under her breath.

"Have any of you seen Milo?" I ask.

A member of the kitchen staff walks by with a tray of drinks and I stop him long enough to graciously take one. When I turn back, Jesse is frowning, eyes focused on the other side of the room. My gaze settles on Savannah who sees the same thing, and it's apparently just as upsetting for her as it is for Jesse.

Looking over my shoulder, I don't see anyone immediately and face forward again. "What's up guys?"

Jesse nods once in the direction as Savannah points. Her amethyst eyes are full of apology, which confuses me even more. With a sigh, I turn around and give the room a better look.

So far, it's a mix of students and faculty mingling together. Lady Alene slowly makes her way through the room, visiting each of the students with a lively smile that almost makes one forget she's made of stone.

I see Milo, grinning. My lips pull up at the corners until the person standing in front of them moves and I see Agatha. Hanging onto Milo. Again. What's more disturbing is Milo appears to be happy about it?

I shake my head and squeeze my eyes shut.

No. Nope. Nuh-uh. This is a trick.

But when I open my eyes, the image is just the same.

Facing Jesse, I narrow my gaze on him. "Not funny."

He meets my gaze and there's a flash of confusion. "I'm not doing that. Even I have lines I would never cross. This is one of them."

I nod. "Okay, so what gives?"

"Are you positive you had no idea about this?" Savannah asks.

I press my lips together as my shoulders start to ache from the building tension within them. "Not a clue. We were fine just yesterday."

I had spent some time with him in his lab helping him kill spiders and set some things up. Nothing happened that would make him angry enough to ignore me, much less cozy up toward Agatha of all people. Seeing him with Agatha, so happy, it hurts. And it's inexplicable. This is not like Milo. Not. At. All.

I glance over my shoulder again and see the smile has yet to fade from my sexy nerd's handsome face.

Ugh.

"What are you going to do?" Jesse asks. "I'll hold his arms and you can punch?"

I shake my head. "I think we can all agree whoever that is, it isn't Milo."

"Well, he looks an awful lot like him," Savannah adds as she continues to stare in disbelief.

"Never going to know standing around here," Jesse mentions.

I nod. "You're right." Without another word, I spin on my heels and march my way toward the two. Approaching like a madwoman is probably not the best idea, so halfway across the arena, I slow down, evening out my pace and focusing on my breathing.

Three quarters of the way there, Agatha spots me, smile fading as she tightens her grip around Milo's arm. And he just stands there and acts like nothing is wrong with this picture. His eyes rest on mine and his smile also falls, fading into a frown. He clears his throat and appears rather displeased at my standing in front of him. I glance at Agatha again, noticing a ruby red pendant dangling from her neck by a golden chain that starts to glow as I get closer.

Instinctively, she clutches the stone and tucks it protectively into her silky blouse.

I stop in front of them and force myself to ignore the pain stabbing at my heart with Milo's reaction. "What's going on, and what are you doing hanging on my boyfriend?"

Milo groans and rolls his eyes.

I quirk an eyebrow.

Yeah… there is definitely something up here. Milo would never, *ever* do that. It's like he has a completely different personality. My magic still reacts to him, which is a good sign, but it's diluted. Almost like something's diminishing the strength of our connection.

Agatha shrugs. "Maybe he's had a change of heart. People can change. Right, Milie-poo?"

Milie-poo? Of all the pet names she could come up with, *that* is what she decided to go with?

I shove the urge to gag and roll my eyes.

"Precisely," Milo says and sets an annoyed glare on me.

It's like he doesn't even know me.

"Just because we share a few classes doesn't make us friends," he adds, and it's like pouring salt into an open wound.

I take a few moments to gather my thoughts and breathe through the pain. My attention moves to Agatha who smiles triumphantly at me, and that's almost enough to make me crumble. I've taken ridicule and humiliation from boorish trolls, but Milo speaking to me in that way cut me to the quick. And damn Agatha for standing there gloating over it. But I refuse to give her the satisfaction of seeing me visibly upset, despite how I really feel inside. She will not see a damn bit of hurt from me.

"Have a nice day now, Wren," she says.

My hands clench into fists as anger overwhelms everything in my body. I stare daggers at Agatha and want nothing more than to beat her into a bloody pulp.

Jesse's hand cups my shoulder, and I suck in a deep calming breath. Thank the gods for that. As much as I want to wipe that smirk from Agatha's smug face and shake the hell out of Milo, I have to be smart about this. I certainly don't have to handle this on my own. I have a team that backs me. Though Milo has been a part of my team for some time, it's clear he's not himself right now.

I nod and switch my gaze from Agatha to Milo. His eyes flash with the light of recognition. It's so subtle that I almost didn't catch it before it was gone as quickly as it showed. Had I not been looking at him, I would have missed it. But it's all the confirmation I need. The real Milo is still in there somewhere. And judging by the overly confident look on Agatha's face, she knows what's going on, and she's behind it all.

I know it deep in my bones.

Agatha looks up at Milo. "Let's go find our friends."

Milo nods once and leads Agatha through the room. I narrow my gaze on Agatha's back as she sashays through the room, knowing full and well she thinks she has won.

Well I got news for her. She just messed with the wrong mage.

Jesse tugs on my shoulder and I snap my attention toward him. He flinches, lifting his hand off my shoulder and into the air as if surrendering. "Whoa, killer."

I soften a bit. "Sorry. That woman just grates on my nerves."

He nods, shoving his hands into his pockets. "I see that."

Savannah joins us. "So, that looks like it went well."

I face her. "Not the word I would use, but if it weren't for Jesse recognizing I was about to boil over, there would be a blood bath."

Her amethyst eyes widen. "Well it's a good thing Jesse stepped in. So… what's the deal?"

OLIVIA ASH

"Something is wrong. I know it. He acted like he didn't even know me."

Her eyebrows draw together.

"He didn't even appear to see me. I'm hurt." Jesse looks after the direction Milo and Agatha went and I can tell that he isn't joking. He's worried too.

I shake my head. "We need to figure out what she did to him."

"How do you know it's her?" Savannah asks.

"I saw a flash in Milo's eyes. It was like he recognized me and looked at me the same way he always looks at me... until today. I read about something like this happening when someone's under certain types of enchantments. And seeing that Agatha's got her grimy little claws in him, I'm certain she's behind it."

"Family pow-wow?" Jesse asks as he slips his arm comfortingly around my waist.

I smile, loving that he referred to the team as a family. Because, to me, we are. "Damn right."

"I'll get Soren. You guys hunt down Gideon. Meet you at his office in ten?" Savannah offers.

We nod and move through the room on the hunt for the headmaster.

CHAPTER TEN

We find Gideon talking with some of the dignitaries. Lady Alene is standing near him. We casually approach and Lady Alene's gaze turns to me. She softly smiles.

"Happy Patron Mage Day, Lady Alene," I say.

"Thank you, Wren. Are you enjoying the festivities?"

I nod. "They are beautiful. The events showing on the canvases out in the halls are amazing. Better than watching a movie. You were quite the fierce warrior in your time."

She laughs. "Indeed. I was."

I face Gideon. "Headmaster Storm, I have a concern about a student. When you have a moment, can you please see me?"

He nods. "Give me a moment, and I'll pull away to address this concern."

I nod.

Moments later, he stands with me and Jesse in a quiet corner of the room. After letting him know something is wrong with Milo and we need to talk, he nods and asks us to meet him in his office. With a pang of regret over leaving Lady Alene's celebration so prematurely, we slip out of the arena and head down the hall.

At least I was able to say hi and show my respect and admiration for her.

But I'm sure Lady Alene would usher us to Gideon's office upon hearing what's going on with Milo.

We didn't have to wait long until the headmaster was with us, Savannah and Soren flanking him.

"What's the problem with Milo?" Gideon asks as he takes his seat at his desk.

I twist to face the room in my favorite perch on the windowsill. "He's different. Personality and all."

"He's also suddenly okay with Agatha hanging onto him," Savannah adds. "She's enchanting him in some way."

Gideon frowns.

Soren stands straight from leaning against the wall

behind Gideon's desk. "What do you mean? He was fine yesterday."

"I know," I say. "That's exactly what I said."

"Tell me everything you've noticed," Gideon says.

I spill everything. The cold manner in which he responded to my presence, the strange flash of recognition in Milo's eyes where it looked like he was warring with something inside. The proud and triumphant smirk Agatha flashed. Every little detail that I thought would help point us in the right direction to figuring out what is going on with my sexy nerd.

"He literally acted like he couldn't be bothered with her," Jesse says as he finalizes his own account of what he observed.

"Right. Even went as far as to tell me that just because we share a few classes together, it doesn't make us friends." My voice gives out at the end. Because if anything, we were more than friends. So much more. We share a bond. One I thought was unbreakable. I clear my throat. "He's in there. I know it. I feel it."

"You're saying your magic still reacts to his?" Soren asks.

"Barely," I mutter. "It's almost like something is blocking it. Diluting the potency."

Gideon nods, jotting down notes on a piece of paper in front of him. "Excellent observations. What else can you tell me about Agatha?"

I shrug. "She was protective over a necklace she didn't want me to see. I've never seen her wear it until today. She flaunted Milo in front of me like a carrot. Acted like she won whatever game she's been playing at."

"Savannah?" Gideon asks, lifting his gaze to her.

She shrugs. "I don't know any more than what they already told you, but I will do everything I can to help figure out what is going on. Maybe I can play detective and befriend her just to get closer. It's a long shot, but one worth taking."

"See what you can glean from her at a distance. If she's behind Milo's change, I would hate for you to succumb to it as well."

"Now that would be interesting to see." Jesse wriggles his eyebrows.

I scowl at him. This is not the time for jokes.

"I'll be careful. I may have to pull away from you," she says to me. "At least for a while. Until I can get the information I need. It may help if she doesn't see us together as often. Make it look like we had a falling out."

My heart sinks at that thought. But for Milo, it is a

small sacrifice to pretend I don't have a best friend for a while. I nod.

"What about calling Milo in?" Soren asks. "We can leave, and you can talk to him privately, Gideon."

I stand from the window and walk toward the middle of the room. "I am not leaving. I'll remain out of sight, but I want to be here so we can all get down to the bottom of this."

"What about our special room?" Jesse nods toward the magical closet.

Our secret training spot is the perfect way to get Milo alone. Problem is, if he has any sort of allegiance to Agatha, that could spell trouble for us. "We can hide in it or you can talk to Milo in it?"

"Hide, of course." Jesse smirks deviously. "Or better yet, we could just tie him up and keep him in there. Throw in a few herbology books for him to pass the time while he detoxes from Agatha."

Is it bad that I actually think this is a plausible idea?

Gideon clears his throat. "Let's first make it look like I'm calling him in to discuss a class matter with him. We can look into other options as needed in the future."

We all nod. He sends a note and it materializes into a megaphone. It floats through the air and toward wherever Milo is. Likely still at the celebration with Agatha attached to his arm.

I shudder at the thought.

"While we wait, you four go into the closet." Gideon stands and walks to the secret room. He taps on the door a few times and clicks his fingers in a rhythmic fashion. He opens the door and faces us, gesturing for us to enter.

Once we're all filed in, he closes the door and it dematerializes. He stands in front of us, staring at a spot almost as though he can't see us. "I can't see you, but you can see and hear everything. Try not to make a sound."

The four of us nod. Even though he can't see it.

Strangely enough, he nods once then heads to his desk.

We don't have to wait long before there's a knock on the door.

"Enter," Gideon announces.

The door opens and Agatha and Milo enter.

Sheesh, can't the woman give the man five minutes to attend to a matter that doesn't even involve her? My patience has run out with her, and if it weren't for Soren and Jesse each grabbing an arm to keep me from barging through the secret door, I would have already made good on my promise.

"Miss Collins, I asked for Milo. This doesn't involve you. Please, wait outside for him."

I chuckle under my breath. That's my sexy headmaster. She wouldn't dare disobey him. Not if she wants to stay in this school and near my Milo.

She giggles and bats at the air. "Oh, it's okay. Whatever you have to say to Milie-poo can be said in front of me. We don't keep secrets. Right, snuggly bear?"

Gods this woman is insufferable with her vomit-inducing pet names. Milo would never stand for them. Yet another reason why I know she did something to him.

"Right." Milo doesn't even blink. He's just... going with it.

"Be that as it may," Gideon insists, "this is a confidential meeting."

"He said I can stay." Her smile fades a little. She's quick to recover her façade though. Bouncing blond curls and all.

"Miss Collins, I'll put it to you this way. You can either leave and wait for him outside, or you can continue to disobey my direct order and suffer a suspension. Either way, you will be leaving his side. One just ends sooner than the other."

Damn I wish I could see Gideon's face right now.

As it is, his voice sounds rigid. It's hot as hell to see him putting his foot down.

Agatha shrugs as though she wasn't just walking a thin line with the man in charge of her place here at the academy. "Fine." She leans into Milo, smiling and batting her bright blue eyes. "I'll be waiting for you right outside the door."

"You'll be waiting a while," Gideon adds.

She pouts at him with an icy cold glare.

"I'll see you soon," Milo says and pulls away from Agatha.

For the first freaking time in the whole evening, I breathe a sigh of relief.

Agatha casts a quick look over her shoulder before she walks out the door, and to say that she looks less than thrilled is an understatement. However, I smirk with my own triumph. She's out of the picture, if only for the moment.

"Have a seat," Gideon's hand gestures to one of the seats stationed in front of his desk.

Milo nods and takes one of the seats. "What can I do for you, Headmaster Storm?"

Now that is another fact and clue to Milo not being himself. He would only ever refer to Gideon formally if he was in the presence of other students. Never behind closed doors.

"One of your peers reached out to me with a concern about your health and well-being. I'm following up on that report."

Milo nods once. His expression is an emotionless, stony mask. It's bizarre. I don't like this new Milo. I do not like him one bit. I want my Milo back. He doesn't express any of his normal mannerisms. No shoving his glasses up his nose. No running his hand through his hair. It's like he's a robot.

Just another point that proves just how much is not right.

I bite the corner of my lower lip and lean into Soren's chest. His arm instinctively wraps around my torso, and I find comfort within the never-ending warmth that seeps into my skin. Jesse rubs my left arm, providing additional comfort, and I'm ever grateful for them both being here with me.

"Anything you want to tell me?" Gideon asks, and there's almost a hint of desperate worry in his tone that makes me stand straighter.

"Not that I can think of. Who made the report?" Milo asks.

"It was anonymous, I'm afraid."

Watching Milo and his interaction with the headmaster, it's almost like he's on autopilot, completely unemotional. No spark of the real Milo is visible, probably buried somewhere deep inside—if at all. And that makes my heart hurt.

"No unusual illnesses, nightmares, or delusions?" Gideon presses.

Milo shakes his head. "None I can think of."

"Tell me about your relationship with Agatha," Gideon continues. "How long have you been... dating?"

"I don't recall."

Red flags are flying all over this. His response just doesn't make sense. How can you not remember when you stopped being you and changed into this brand of Milo? His memory is always spot on. Always. Him not remembering is not a good sign.

"It's some type of mind-control spell," Savannah whispers from behind me. "That's what is affecting him. Now we can move forward with a plan."

I nod. "Well, this is a start." Although I'm grateful we now have a direction to go in, something tells me fixing this mess won't be easy. But, there's hope for him yet. Now it's just about narrowing down the list of spells and going from there.

"We will have to hurry," Soren adds, his whisper deep and full of warning. "If he's this bad already, that means it's a powerful spell, and it's getting worse."

Great. Now there is a time limit. One which does

nothing good for my increasing anger for the bitch out in the hall. Once we figure out what's wrong with Milo, she's gonna have a rude awakening coming for her.

Girl has messed with the wrong mage.

After what seems like forever, Gideon sighs. He's not getting very far with Milo, and there's only so much he can do at this time. "All right. You may go."

Milo quickly stands from his seat.

"First," Gideon says, stopping Milo from rushing out the door and back to Agatha. "Please come to me if you need anything."

He nods once, still unaffected, before walking out the door. Agatha's back is to the door as it opens. She spins around to face him, face lighting up with joy. A pinch forms in the center of my forehead. I could have sworn there was a look of worry in her eyes.

Good. She should be worried.

Because I'm coming for her.

The door shuts and we all breathe out a heavy sigh.

I exit the closet, Soren, Jesse, and Savannah following after. We all huddle around Gideon's desk as he massages his temples with his eyes closed. A frown pulls his lips down at the corners, and I can tell this whole thing deeply troubles him. Milo's our team-mate. Part of the family. And now he's in trouble.

"Well what does the wise headmaster think?" Jesse asks.

He shakes his head. "Nothing good. It's almost like his soul is being erased. I can't see it. There's a black shroud covering him."

"I noticed that too just now," Savannah says. "I can't look into his past, present, or future."

If I wasn't concerned enough, I most certainly am now. "I'm going to make Agatha pay for this."

Gideon holds up a hand. "Let's not be hasty. We need a plan. That is the best way to help."

I nod. "Okay. I'll reach out to Professor Crosswell. She is a master at this sort of thing."

"Excellent idea." Gideon leans back in his chair.

"I'll do some mischief of my own," Jesse adds. "Reconnaissance is a favorite of mine."

"I'll discreetly test Agatha's merit, as well as keep an eye on Milo," Soren says. "Maybe I'll have him perform random duties for me, keep him busy and as far away from that girl as possible."

I love it. We're all protective over him.

A letter burns to life on his desk. Gideon quickly reads it. Something in that letter is disconcerting to my handsome headmaster. He frowns as worry creases his forehead.

"What's wrong?" I ask.

He settles his gaze on me and briefly flits his eyes to Savannah before settling on the letter. He takes a deep breath. "It's the pathology report from the feral harpy eagle you and Soren killed. It was infected with the plague."

My heart skips a beat as my worries shift to my father and his safety. "My dad."

Gideon nods. "Already on top of it."

I release the breath I had been holding. "Good. Thank you."

He levels his gaze on me. "You're both incredibly lucky you didn't contract the disease. That was close."

"What are you going to do now?" Soren asks.

"Visit our friend, Lionel. He requested we speak urgently." He stands and makes his way around his desk. "I'll let you know when I'm back."

I nod. "Be careful."

"Of course." He rubs my back gently as we walk toward the door.

The creature had the disease and came to me and Soren on the island just days before the year started. If one got away, how many more? And how long before this storm really does hit the island?

CHAPTER ELEVEN

The door to Professor Crosswell's room is closed, but there is a collection of banging and loud cursing coming from the other side. The window that reveals the room is covered with black paper decorated with a glittery symbol. It looks like a small circle, within a square that sits in the bottom of a triangle, all housed within a larger, all encompassing, circle. A slight golden glow resonates from the image.

Despite the enchanting nature the strange symbol has, I hesitate outside the door, not wanting to disturb the woman when she's already in a foul mood. Still, I need to. This may be a bad time, but I have to help Milo, and she's one of the best in her field. Taking in a deep breath, I let it out slowly and knock on the door.

"Yes, come in!" She sounds irritated by my interruption.

Considering the reason I'm here, she's going to have to deal with it.

Squaring my shoulders, I twist the knob and open the door. On any other day, I'd probably slip away and give her some space. But not today. Milo is in need, whether he recognizes that or not. And thus, I'm here on his behalf. If anyone can help with his strange malady, it's Professor Crosswell.

I walk through the doorway and instantly pause. Her office is like a small research lab. Vials filled with red liquid lay in a neat row on a tray. Machines and microscopes fill a large table. I barely get a chance to take in the sheer level of various things cluttering the desk when Professor Crosswell snatches my attention.

"Ms. Blackwood, I'm incredibly busy, so if this isn't an emergency, later would be better." She brushes her long, dark-brown hair from her face.

I nod. "It *is* important, actually."

"Is someone bleeding from their eyes?" She levels her stern gaze on me.

"Well, no... but—"

"Then come back later. I'm busy." She continues on to her notebook and starts scribbling furiously on the page.

I huff out my own annoyance. "Milo is under some sort of spell and needs help."

She points a finger at the row of bookshelves on the opposite side of the room. "Help yourself. If I had a dime for every time some juvenile magical prank has been pulled, I'd be a millionaire by now."

I glance at the shelves then level my gaze on the woman as frustration quickly grows within me. This isn't like one of Jesse's little brothers and their pranks. "What are you working on that's more important than helping a student?"

She breathes out a long sigh before leaning back in her seat. Seeming to regain a sense of calm, she gestures toward three vials standing upright in a rack. Two of them are bright red, and one is black.

"While you and your classmates are enjoying the protections this island affords, I'm trying to help the magusari reverse engineer a cure for that damned plague. All three of those vials are samples of infected blood from recent victims, and the black one happens when they die. When we've failed to cure them."

A pang of worry hits me as I remember Savannah's father and brothers. I hope they're staying safe on the front lines, fighting this disease. My heart fell in my chest when my best friend told me how her father accepted the very real possibility that he would contract the plague and refused to visit with his daughter. If the magusari is enlisting the aid of Professor Crosswell to quickly reach a cure, they must have faith in her. It means she's good at what she does.

And if that's the case, then maybe she can shut up and let me get a word in for Milo. She can help him too.

"So," I say, eyeing the black vial. "You really are one of the consultants the magusari council is using. Have you made any progress?"

She taps her nail against the surface of her desk, frowning at the dark vial with its congealed, poisonous blood. "As you can see by my frustration, I have not. We are running out of time."

I approach but decide not to sit in the seat across from her. There's no way I want to be too close to a plague sample. "Then you've probably already heard about the infected harpy eagle from Crimson Isles?"

Her jaw drops slightly, and she leans forward. "A harpy eagle? Infected?"

Oops. I guess she hadn't heard.

"Look, I probably shouldn't have said anything..."

"This changes everything." She jumps up and starts crossing out formulas and calculations in her notebook.

"Professor, I just wanted to see if you could help with Milo."

"Find whatever you think is useful and leave. I don't have *time*." She reaches for something on her desk and accidentally knocks over her cup of coffee. She groans, frustrated with the liquid mess now covering her research. "Please, Wren. Take the books and go!"

Fine. I can take them with me to the library and start researching. I'll pull one of the guys to help if I need it.

I storm over to the bookshelf and look over the titles etched on the spines, picking out a few that I think will help point us further in the right direction if not solve our problem quickly. I cradle the books in my arms and start for the door.

"Ms. Blackwood," Professor Crosswell says, soaking up the spilled coffee from her desk with a yellow rag. "If it is something serious, then please let the infirmary know. I just need to handle this first. Understand?"

I narrow my eyes at her and simply nod once.

Walking out of the office, I'm frustrated and irritated that someone who's supposed to put her students first is more concerned with her experiment. At the same time, I can't completely blame her. I understand that she's stressed out working on finding a cure for the plague, like so many other mages. But damn it, this is my Milo, and he needs help too.

As I storm through the halls, I head for the library. I pay little attention to the statues, the view of the island from the windows, or thestudents who grumble at me to watch where I'm going. My number one focus is figuring out what is wrong with Milo sooner rather than later.

It may be hard to sit in the library, especially considering that's where Milo and I first met, but I have to identify the spell he's been hit with in order to move forward. That's at least one thing I learned from Professor Crosswell. I can clear my head and dig into the few books I've taken from the professor's room. I can start with spells matching Milo's symptoms and go from there. That would be good.

More importantly, I just want to be alone and think.

Sitting in the library, at my favorite table, I listen to the whispers of other students studying at the tables around me. They're talking about random, everyday things. I miss talking like this with Milo. I also miss the talks about his experiments, his hopes of becoming a great alchemist, and how his family is doing.

Most especially, I miss *him*.

His presence, his smell, the way my magic reacts to his. I miss his beautiful, captivating brown eyes taking in mine. The way he pushes his glasses up his nose or runs his fingers through his hair.

The students sitting a couple of tables over mention some exciting creature they get to study soon. That piques my interest for about thirty seconds, but then it wanes as they trail off and don't go into further detail.

After a few more moments spent processing everything happening to Milo, I turn my attention to the stained-glass window that glows with a golden light, brightening the colors. The whispers still pull at my attention, making me wonder if researching in the library at this time of day is a bad decision. It's hard to focus, but I know time is of the essence. After all, as soon as I find what was used on him, the sooner we can rid him of his ailment along with that woman, Agatha.

I turn my attention to the books and my notes sitting next to them.

The first book is called "Complete Guide to Curses

Based on Symptoms," and has a comprehensive, compiled list of possible curses based on the more typical and widely known symptoms. Its counterpart, a compiled list of spells, curses, and enchanted afflictions, shares a list of symptoms based on the curse that the conjurer is seeking. This helps list what could possibly have been done to Milo.

However, Milo's symptoms, from what I noticed, don't entirely match up with any of the spells or curses I've seen. His symptoms, based on my observation are loss of energy, paleness, and he appears to be suffering from loss of sleep. Now, while many curses will cause those things, what sticks out to me the most is Milo's frightening lack of mental clarity. It's as if a thick fog has overtaken his mind and he's given up his will.

Worst of all, I don't feel his magic the way I used to.

It's like a wall has been erected to separate us, and the only image burning in my mind right now is that smug-faced little brat Agatha.

I shake my head and try looking at another curse listed. I have a feeling there is more to uncover. Hmm, this one mentions a lack of appetite, but I have yet to observe this. Bitterly, I think of how little of Milo I've been able to see. I move on other symptoms, like mood change, personality changes. The closest I've been to a possible answer is mind control spells which are covered in my third borrowed book. But even then, nothing adds up enough for it to explain everything. And with magic, everything is always precise. Everything must line up exactly, or it's not a fit. It's not the answer.

So, though I know that the curses and spells I've researched are definitely not ones that Milo has, I am still no closer to finding an answer.

I sigh and plop my head onto the table and try to think of what this means.

In a way, this is a blessing in disguise. Just because Milo doesn't have the spells listed in either of these books doesn't mean all hope is lost. We just checked two books off the list. So, theoretically, it's a good thing he doesn't have these.

On the other hand, since nothing here in these books adds up, chances are, it's not a typical spell, and that probably means something forbidden and dark was used on him. That definitely is *not* a blessing. Still, that means searching in the restricted section could lead me to exactly what I need. I hate the idea of it. I almost want to find an excuse to avoid the restricted section, but it's the only thing that makes sense.

I have to find a way in. I have to find that curse.

I stand up and walk toward the door. I know I won't be able to actually get into this part of the library. No one can without permission. But I am intending to pull a Jesse and sneak my way in anyway. I want to look inside and see if there is anything that stands out. Missing books, something that's out of place. Anything. Perhaps a book will jump out at me and sing that it's the one I've been looking for.

Hey, it could happen.

As I draw closer, I hear someone shuffling about behind the door. Narrowing my eyes on the wooden barrier that seals away all the interesting and forbidden things, I peek in through the iron slats covering the window, only to find that the room is basked in shadow and not so much as a candle flame flickers. I can't see anyone in there. But I know someone is. No sooner than I lift my hand to knock on the door, a megaphone appears in front of me.

"Wren Blackwood, report to Professor McCallister's office immediately."

I turn on my heel and rush out, cursing under my breath that I've been pulled away at the worst time.

Whatever Soren has to tell me, it had better be important.

CHAPTER TWELVE

Soren's office comes into view as I snake my way through the crowd of students moving to their next class or heading to their House. I swear if I see Milo with Agatha, I'm going to knock that girl into next week. I'm still on edge after Professor Crosswell practically shoved me out of her office. So, my patience to deal with irritating, spoiled rich bitches is slim to none.

I hope Soren has some good news regarding our plan.

As I continue on, someone taps my shoulder, and I turn to find Savannah smiling at me.

"Hey, where you off to?" I ask.

"Same place as you."

I don't bother asking her how she knows where I'm

going. I've learned she is good at just knowing things. Her power is the ability to see things, like mini stories in people. She picks up on stuff most don't even realize about themselves and she can sometimes see the future.

I nod.

I feel Jesse before I see him. Soon, he bumps into me with a mischievous smile. "Don't tell me you two got yourselves into trouble and didn't bother inviting me."

"Who said anything about being in trouble?" Savannah asks, staring at him with an accusatory expression.

"We're on our way to see Soren," I add. "Where are you heading?"

His face twists into a mask of confusion. "Same."

"I wonder what's going on for all three of us to be called to his office like this?" I ask.

"Perhaps Milo is playing hard to get and Soren needs our help to lasso him in," Jesse says. There's a dangerous glint in his eyes as I glance at him. It's almost as if he already has a list of ideas and is sorting out the steps he'll need to take in order to make his plan smoother.

Sometimes, he unsettles me when he does that.

Savannah shrugs. "I would tell you if I knew."

"No, you wouldn't." I interject. I add a smile to let her know I'm just playing. Sort of.

She winks. "But maybe Soren wants to update us regarding the information Gideon received the other day. My father had warned me the disease was getting worse and spreading. Maybe it's a plan of action he wants to make us aware of."

"Well, let's not keep the man waiting." Jesse steps between me and Savannah and pushes his way through the thinning crowd of people in the halls, stopping at the door before waving us forward. "He's impatient enough as it is and nearly impossible to please."

"Just for you," I say with a wink.

"So pushy sometimes," Savannah says.

"You get used to it," I say. "Eventually."

Once we're all inside the room, Soren stands from his desk and walks toward the door. "We have a little field trip to the gardens."

"Then why not have us just meet you there?" I ask.

"I'll explain once we get there. We don't have a lot of time." He opens the door leading out of the room. "Follow along now, students."

He faces us with his serious professor expression and acts like a pissed off man as he storms out the door.

"Well, this is going to be fun." Jesse smirks as we follow Soren back out of the office.

Fun is not the term I would use to describe following Soren anywhere when he's in a foul mood. If anything, this gives me a less than fun reminder of what it's like to be on his bad side.

As we walk through the hall, I cross my arms over my chest, wondering just what the hell is going on. Jesse walks as though he isn't bothered by anything, and Savannah has an even expression as she moves quietly along.

For all intents and purposes, we look like we just got caught breaking some rules and are on our way to our punishment.

It dawns on me that is exactly what Soren is aiming for, and I go along with it.

As we make it to the garden, Soren veers to the right, walking deep into the wooden grove. Jesse and I exchange a concerned glance. This is a whole lot of walking for something that was supposed to take place in the gardens. We passed them, now what is the plan?

Something tells me, I'm not going to like this answer.

"Are you going to tell us what this is about now?" I ask Soren's back.

"Quiet!" His sharp tone unsettles me and makes me consider perhaps this isn't all for show.

Still, I glare at his back. The handsome asshole. I sincerely hope he has a good excuse for this type of response. Otherwise, we're going to be exchanging some not so nice words.

Soon, we arrive at a small meadow, coated in a fine dusting of snow. Lady Alene stands silently, waiting for what I hope is an explanation of what the hell is going on. Soren holds up his hand, signaling us to stop. He takes another couple of steps forward and rakes his eyes over our surroundings. Finally, he settles his serious amber gaze on Jesse. "A little privacy, please?"

Jesse simply nods.

Instantly, I see a slight shimmer appear around us, growing from the ground up. Had he not trained me to search for illusions, I would have missed out on the pretty glittering invisible wall that rises up above us, sealing us in a soft dome. Inside, nothing has changed. Outside, to anyone who would happen past, would only see an empty meadow.

Once finished, Jesse winks at me. "Wish granted."

I smile and shake my head. Such a handsome joker.

Lady Alene steps forward, holding out a letter toward me. "I apologize for the secrecy, but times are changing here, and we needed to be extra careful. Tuck this away and read it later. Once you are finished, burn it so that there is no evidence."

I nod and take the letter. But the level of confusion is only rising. "Thank you."

She nods as she steps back and lets Soren take over.

"Gideon is in trouble."

I gasp. "What do you mean 'in trouble'?" I tuck the letter into my back pocket. "Why do I have to wait to read this, again?"

"Because Gideon requested it," Lady Alene says.

That's good enough for me. He must have a good reason for me to wait. Judging by Soren's rush to get us here, it's pretty damn important.

"Why isn't Gideon here?" I ask.

"We'll get to that in just a moment," Lady Alene says.

I nod and turn my gaze back to Soren. I don't like it, but I trust they'll explain what's going on.

"The Order has infiltrated the Council. We don't know how high up it goes or for how long they've been entrenched among us. They must feel emboldened, because they're using the council's power to investigate Gideon and you." Soren's eyes take in mine, and I see the need to protect me burning within them.

Gideon and me. That can only mean one thing.

Someone has tipped off the council about our relationship being more than professional.

Fan-freaking-tastic.

"How do you know?" My mouth suddenly goes dry and my heart skips a beat. If they are launching an investigation now, that means Gideon's position as headmaster is at stake, and this is going to equal a whole lot of unpleasantries.

"Remember Captain Lionel Rhodes?" he asks.

I nod. "He's the captain we spoke to about the harpy eagle on Crimson Isles."

"That's how we found out about this."

I shake my head. "That doesn't make sense. How does *he* know?"

"It's his job." Soren pinches the bridge of his nose like this whole mess is taking a lot more time to explain than he cares to give. But I don't care, I need to know, especially since now I'm most definitely involved.

"And what exactly is his job? I may not be magusari, but this mess obviously involves me. If I'm part of this, along with Gideon, I have a right to know exactly what and why. Now, spill." I take a couple firm steps closer, keeping my gaze locked on him. Unwavering. If he thinks a simple explanation is going to be enough, then he's got another thing coming.

Soren sighs. "Woman, we don't have time for a long, detailed story. The gist of it is that he's a double agent. The Order thinks he's one of their sycophants vying for a position among them, but he's really working for us. He's the source that's been helping me and Gideon this entire time. That's how he found out about the complaint filed against Gideon. He also knows the Order just gave marching orders to the council infiltrators, and he's working on finding out who they are. Satisfied?"

I nod, meeting his gaze, not bothering to hide my worry. It's beneficial that we have some eyes and ears on our side, but apparently the Order's reach extends farther than we thought. This whole time, we thought we've been winning battles by rescuing my father and taking down my corrupt aunt—but the Order has set its sight on winning the war. I can't let that happen.

They have another thing coming if they think this is the best way to get me to give in and hand myself over to them. But I can also see that now they are pulling out all the stops. And that's just unacceptable.

"What exactly are they investigating?" Savannah asks.

Soren looks at Savannah and has an expression that says she should already know.

"Oh…" Her eyes widen as the realization hits her.

As well as I do. It's the relationship between me and Gideon. It's the fact that we are more than what we should be. And I have an idea on who let slip the secret. Unfortunately, there's nothing I can do about it. They're already dead.

I shake my head as anger begins to boil my blood. "Impossible. How could they possibly know anything? We've been careful."

I totally recognize what's going on, and the Order should know better than to underestimate me. First, Milo. Now Gideon? The Order is trying to take my men away. Whatever spell Agatha cast is beyond the skills of a second-year student, that much I know. What if someone's been helping her, guiding her on what to do?

"It will be okay. Just don't go anywhere alone with Gideon unless there is a third-party present. For the time being anyway," Soren adds. "The investigation is bad enough, and news of it, not to mention the rumors, will spread through the school."

I shake my head.

"Jesse?"

Jesse steps forward and tries to comfort me. And as much as I love him for it, it's not helping. It's not going to magically make the Order back the hell off or suddenly bring Milo back to himself.

Soren huffs. "There will be an investigation. As long as that is ongoing, your interaction with Gideon must be kept to a minimum. Don't give them any more ammunition to use against you."

"You think?" I say looking at him as I start to pace the small area protected by the illusion. The tension is building inside me, and the need to punch the crap out of everything is slowly overwhelming everything else.

"That is not all, dear Wren," Lady Alene says, and her voice is so full of sadness, I stop to study her. She's frowning.

I sigh. "Do I want to ask?"

"No, but you need to know." She nods at Soren.

He clenches his teeth and I can tell this is the part of the bad news that I most definitely will not like. He takes a few deep breaths before he speaks. "He will likely lose his position as headmaster."

And there it is. The exact thing I knew would come of this if our relationship was discovered.

He loves this job.

My lungs deflate as the most damning truth comes to me.

I... I've killed his career.

There is so much more behind this, and I see right through the Order's method.

"This isn't coincidence." Savannah's voice almost sounds distant.

"I thought that very thing," I say, facing Soren. "First Milo is pulled from me by Agatha, and now Gideon's place in my life is hanging by a delicate thread. Something is up."

My mind rakes through all the possibilities of who would out us. Did a professor see Gideon steal a kiss? Did another student stumble upon us and we didn't see? A staff member?

Soren nods. "I know."

"I've always thought sneaking around added a level of spice to every relationship," Jesse says.

I snap my attention to him. My annoyed glare settling on him. "Really?"

He winks.

I shake my head and sigh. My adorable, incredibly sexy jokester needs to hone his timing skills. This isn't it. Though I don't want to admit it right now, he does bring up a good point.

"Look," Soren says, bringing the attention back to him. "This is only temporary."

"But how did they find out?" I ask, wondering if it could've been anyone other than the one person I suspect.

"I don't know the answer to that. A report was

made. That's all I know." Soren holds out his hand toward me. I take it, and he pulls me in close.

"Let me guess, we have to be more careful now too?" I ask, my words muffled in his chest.

He kisses the top of my head. "We all have to be extremely careful about what steps we take from here on. For now, all we can do is continue with our plan of helping Milo. I'll keep an eye on the situation with Gideon."

I roll my eyes and clench fistfuls of his shirt in my hands. "Fine. But I'm far from happy with this."

"Don't worry, I can keep you warm," Jesse says.

I pull away from Soren and chuckle. "I know you can, but that's not what I mean."

"We will make it through this. All of us," Soren says with a nod to Jesse and Savannah.

"You're damn right. One way or another, I'm going to get to the bottom of this. No one messes with my men, my team, or my family."

CHAPTER THIRTEEN

I make it back to my room, feeling less than thrilled with the news. The letter sitting in my back pocket has been burning a hole through me since I placed it there. Once I'm finally behind my closed door, I let out a long sigh and pull out the letter.

I scan it at first to confirm it's in Gideon's handwriting. I run my finger over the words, wishing different choices had been made. I hate that he's faced with losing his job for simply following his heart. I want to make this right.

With a deep breath, I read the words.

Dearest Wren,

By now, you have learned the news of the investigation of our relationship. I apologize for not being there or delivering the news myself. I wish I had been. However, with the circumstances being as they currently are, it risks too much.

Know this, regardless of what happens, I will remain by your side. Through thick and thin. I pledge myself to you, and only you.

If you can forgive me for the way the news was delivered to you, wait until the stroke of midnight. Sneak out of your room (I know, I'm asking you to break the rules), and portal to my estate, where you will be safe and away from prying eyes. I'll be waiting for you there. We won't have much time, thanks to the investigation, but coming to me at my estate will at least let me partially make up for not being there when I should have been.

Whatever happens, I remain yours.

Gideon.

Oh, my sweet, sweet, ridiculously handsome man. His words touch me in ways I never knew were possible. My heart breaks for him and how worried he must be right now thinking the absolute worst.

Per the instructions I was given, and much to my dismay, I stand and walk to the fireplace and set the letter inside. Using my magic, I burn every bit of it until there is nothing left but a charred stain on the stone.

I stand and stare at the spot his letter occupied just moments ago and recall the beautiful words that almost sang to me from off the page. Of course, I'm going to go see him. I'm not heartless. With a smile tugging on my lips, I turn to prepare.

Midnight can't come soon enough.

Once midnight strikes, I dress in the darkest clothes I can find to blend into the shadows. I make my way through the halls of the castle, tip-toeing my way along the stone floors, careful not to make a sound. I slip past the kitchens. As I rush past the door, I notice Caseus is up late. That makes me stop and poke my head into the doorway.

Oddly enough, he's not cooking or cleaning. He's fumbling through a stack of books. I narrow my eyes, wondering what a cook would be doing just hanging out browsing books. He checks his watch, sighing impatiently and looking toward the door. I duck out of the way, just in time to avoid being seen, but that's my cue to leave. He's obviously waiting for someone to show up, and that is clearly not me.

Once outside, I take a path that winds its way through the gnome garden. Several gnomes are spread throughout the garden, diligently working. I chuckle at the cute miniature lamps some of them are carrying while others toil in the garden. I had always wondered what they were up to, because during the day it seemed they didn't do much.

They start to grumble and indignantly raise their fists at me when I accidentally trample a few flowers. And these little bastards can be shrill and loud. I decide that it's too risky to hang around. As much as I love seeing them rush to and fro, their yelling will bring unwanted attention. And, needless to say, I am a woman on a mission.

Besides, I have no idea who is watching me, and it could be all the wrong people. I need to do this quickly and quietly. No gnomes.

I pick up my pace and finish my trek toward the southern shore of the island, making sure to double check that I'm alone and wasn't followed before forming my portal.

I keep my destination in mind, picturing the back deck overlooking the wide, open land surrounded by thick trees. I envision the pitch of the ceiling, the rows of windows, and the smell of the air of the place I have fallen in love with.

Stepping into the glowing column of light, I feel

that familiar tug and immediately step out onto Gideon's estate.

Gideon is waiting for me on his back porch, smiling as I arrive. I run to close the gap between us, rushing into his open arms and slamming into his warm, firm muscled body. He squeezes me to him, and I breathe in deep his scent. Pulling away slightly, I lift up on my toes and press my lips to his. His kiss is warm and inviting, yet hungry at the same time.

"Hello to you, too," he says, voice deep and gravelly.

I chuckle. My head swims with his scent and the taste of his lips.

He pulls me inside and we make our way to the living room. I take a seat on the sofa and he takes the spot next to me, resting his arm on the back of the couch as he leans in a little closer.

"How are you handling everything?" I ask, nearly shrinking under the invisible finger pointed at me. He would never tell me himself, but I know deep down I'm partly responsible for his position being on the line.

He shrugs. "I've been through a lot worse. Has Soren explained what's going on?"

"Yes. I think he's having a hard time with it as well."

He nods. "He blames himself."

"Why?"

"He's him. Soren's basic need is to protect. When that's threatened, he takes it personally."

"I've noticed that a number of times." I recall the story he shared with me. The one about Nadia. He still carries that burden.

"I want to explain everything so that you are aware and don't run into any surprises." He smirks knowingly.

I chuckle. "You know me so well."

"I pay attention." He shifts, twisting in his seat to face me. I do the same as he searches for the right words to begin with. "The magusari have a couple of double-agents. One of them is the man you met in the infirmary."

I nod. "Lionel Rhodes—Soren told me. Just not how he found out."

"A report was made." Gideon offers.

"By who?" I ask, feeling the anger from the initial news rising again.

"Your aunt." His eyes rest on mine, and there's so much emotion in them.

I shake my head in shame.

I knew it.

Deep down, I knew it was her. "I'm so sorry."

Even from the grave, the woman is still causing trouble for me. I know exactly what this is in reference to. The time when she and I faced off on Crimson Isles and Gideon was a tad bit overprotective. My aunt saw right through it, picking up on tells Gideon didn't mean to give away.

That's the only time it could have happened. No one else had been around when we shared our moments of affection.

"I'm the one that owes you an apology."

I settle my gaze on Gideon's, a frown pulling down on my lips. "What? No. Don't you dare."

"Hear me out, please." His beautiful blue-greens keep me ensnared, and I can only nod in response. "I knew what the risks were when this all started. I had no illusion in my head that we were going to make it the four years without being caught. I lost my judgment that night and let too much of my feelings show. If anyone is at fault for this, it's me. Especially with how hard things are going to be for you."

I nod. Because he needs this. I don't need to argue with him, play the game of who's right or wrong. I just need to listen and be here for him, because who knows when I'm going to see him again?

He pulls me close and holds me to him for a while. It's a beautiful and peaceful moment that I never want to end. Someday, it won't have to. But for tonight, our time is short, and I want to make the best of the time we have. So, until it does, I enjoy every single moment of this.

My mind rushes through everything happening around me and how the timing of the investigation into Gideon is too coincidental to that of Milo's change.

I pull away from Gideon to look him in his eyes. His beautiful blue-green gaze appears to be searching mine for a hint at what's going on inside my head.

"This isn't a coincidence. If the Order is behind the investigation into you, I'm confident they're connected to what's going on with Milo."

He pauses to think about that, nodding as though things are clicking into place in his head. "That is very possible. I wondered how someone like Agatha had come across the means to control Milo's mind the way she had. When I spoke with him that evening in my office, I could tell that whatever ensnared his mind had a powerful grip on him. Agatha has no way of pulling that off on her own."

"Exactly. I was thinking the same thing."

"I wish I could do more than just agree with you, but my hands are tied. The more are seen together, the more evidence the Order can collect against us."

"Even Soren has to limit his time with me. It's

almost like they are purposefully trying to separate you all from me."

"I know. It's going to be incredibly difficult. We will get through this, though."

I nod. "What can I do to help you?"

"Just go to classes like everything is normal. We'll only be able to see each other when absolutely necessary. We're going to have to play the hand we've been dealt."

Not much change from the norm. I can do this. With my men backing me, either close to me or at a distance, I know we can do this together.

I smile and relax back into him. The comfort of his arms is welcoming and warm and safe.

"How's my father doing?"

"On another scavenging trip to retrieve information he thinks will win the magusari over and help vindicate him."

"What about the information we found out about the young harpy eagle that attacked me and Soren?" I ask, still unable to help myself from worrying about my father, despite his capabilities.

"He's aware and already has a plan set up."

That's my dad. Always thinking ahead. Love that.

"What's the plan?"

"I asked him not to share it with me because I

suspect the Order is watching our every move. The council-infiltrators may even be aware of you being with me now."

I feel my expression fall from intrigue to utter disappointment. "Will they do anything about it?"

He gazes into my eyes, without an ounce of holding back or pretension. "Time will tell. But I'll remain on guard."

"So, by coming here, I may have sealed the fate of your job?"

"It was my choice." He continues to caress my hair. My eyes slowly close as I sit here and breathe in his scent and soak in the comfort of his couch. "I knew what I was getting myself into when I met you. I knew it would be difficult to keep my feelings in check."

I sigh and melt into him a little more, closing my eyes and taking in the moment.

The grandfather clock chimes four times, pulling me from sleep. It's really early in the morning. I didn't even realize I had fallen asleep. I've stayed with my handsome headmaster longer than I probably should have. But I just can't force myself to move away from him. Still groggy, I snuggle into his side, and I drift back to sleep.

The time to leave has passed, and Gideon gently kisses me to wake me up. His gentle touches coax me to come around, and I smile apologetically at him. Once I'm fully awake, he leads me out the back.

With one last hug and kiss goodbye, I portal back to Blackbriar.

I quickly dart into the shadows in case the sound of the portal alerted anyone to my arrival, and I wait as I process through everything that has happened.

Being away from Gideon now, faced with not having him or Milo, makes it hard to walk. It's almost as if my legs don't want to move unless they are getting closer to the two that I can't even touch right now.

I take solace in knowing Jesse and Soren are still around. Sure, I have to be extremely careful with Soren now, but he's still in sight and we can still steal away a little extra time together. Gideon and Milo? They're virtually off-limits to me.

Their absence bothers me the most. It's like being given something your life becomes dependent on and having that ripped away suddenly and without warning. There are huge holes in my life that I notice every second of the day. There's not a minute that goes by without my thoughts crossing them in some way or form. It's almost depressing.

No, it *is* depressing.

But I can't risk the Order seeing me vulnerable. Not now. Not ever.

Nor am I going to just sit back and watch the Order take away everyone I love. I'll do whatever it takes to get my family back. First step is to unchain Milo from Agatha—I need my sexy nerd's smarts and support. Then, it's about time we work on unmasking the Order. I hope Captain Rhodes delivers that information for us soon. If they think they can strike out at us under the cover of shadows, I'll drag their asses out into the light.

Because deep down, I know in my gut what's going on. They are trying to take my men away in an attempt to leave me vulnerable. Leave me defenseless.

Well I got news for them.

I'm not a damsel in distress, and they have another thing coming if they think I'm so easily taken.

CHAPTER FOURTEEN

I'm stuck. And quite frankly, I'm also feeling a little trapped.

Sure, Soren is close by. Jesse too. But with the way I'm being scrutinized, the gods know who, I can't call on them right this minute. I have to figure this one out alone.

Well, I could call on Jesse, but I don't want to pull him away from his homework. Despite his jokester ways, he has a sharp mind and is really doing his best to pass his classes. Besides, a small part of me is paranoid that the Order will target him if they even get an inkling about us.

It's unfortunate, because he's really great at helping me when I need it, and he makes even the biggest issues seem easily overcome.

He's also constantly horny. That delicious, lip-biting release is always a rather nice way to let out steam and tension. But I'm not in the mood.

What I need is to figure out how to save Milo and keep Gideon from losing his position as headmaster of Blackbriar Academy. On that first task, I finished going through the books Professor Crosswell unceremoniously lent me before ushering me out of her office. I came up with six possible ailments, but again, none of them completely matched up with what Milo was going through. I'll have to return the books later and tell Crosswell thanks for nothing. I silently, maybe a little vindictively, wish for another cup of coffee to splatter all over her desk.

I lay on the overstuffed orange leather couch in the House of Phoenix common room and stare at the fire that swirls over the ceiling. The way the different shades of red, orange, yellow, and white dance with each other is calming and hypnotizing.

But this does nothing for figuring out the answer to all the problems.

Sitting up, I stand from the couch as the massive fireplace reignites and make my way to the main House door. My thoughts are filled with pictures of Milo in his current state. And my heart is filled with horror at how quickly his health is declining. It seems like Milo is having his life drained away from him, and I need to stop it. Now.

I walk through the halls toward the kitchens for a snack. Maybe even a potion to help focus my mind. But as I move, I catch sight of Milo, and he's declining so much faster than I realized.

He's a sickly white color, and it seems as though he's gotten paler since the last time I saw him. His eyes have purple circles beneath them, and his irises have faded from their beautiful chocolate brown to a dull umber. My sexy nerd's eyes are lacking all of the life he once had. His clothing sags on his frame, and when he notices that I see him, he ducks into the hall closest to him.

"Oh no you don't," I say under my breath as I try to catch up.

For being a step away from a full-on zombie, he certainly knows how to move fast.

I round the corner and nearly collide with a trio of House of Phoenix students. I hastily apologize and weave through a gaggle of girls and a couple of tall guys who eye me with amusement. When I make a left turn and peer down the hall I thought Milo had gone down, all I see is an empty corridor.

I feel a pang of sorrow mixed with a burning anger. I know he is under the influence of a dark spell and isn't himself, but I feel like *some* part of him should recognize me. Instead, he runs away as if I have the plague.

This is the worst.

Actually, what's worse is that he's missing classes. He should be heading into his next class with that cute grin on his face, ready to learn. But he's avoiding it to avoid me? Avoid class?

I shake my head because I just don't get it.

He *never* misses class.

Knowledge to Milo is like his spice of life. His driving force. It's just ingrained in him. I once jokingly told him that even if the apocalypse was happening all around us, he'd still try to make it to class. Well, it feels like the end of the world to me, if I can't help him. And he doesn't even see it.

More and more of him is fading away, and that kills me inside. I'm powerless to stop it without a cure, forced to watch him become a shell of what he once was.

I groan as my mind struggles to figure out what is wrong with him and how to save him. It's more than a mere spell. It has to be.

It's dark. Powerful. Insidious. And it hijacks the will and mind like nothing I've ever seen. Gideon is right about Agatha not acting alone. To pull off something like that, she needed help.

From what I've seen, Agatha acts like she doesn't even notice the changes he's going through. She's probably just satisfied that she has distanced him from me. Albeit temporarily, whether she wants to fess up to that or not. It's a fact. Even Soren's tasks had unfortunately come to a stop as soon as Milo started showing signs of withering away. But Agatha continues to act like Milo is a pet. A plaything she can use and cast away once she's done with him.

A lump forms in my throat as I consider why Agatha is using a curse. What happened to just using a silly love spell or charm? I would've been just as pissed and ready to kick her ass, but at least I could snap Milo out of it much easier.

I honestly don't know what's eating Milo away. But I do believe in order to find that out, I have to research the restricted books section. I was so close to sneaking in before Soren called me to his office. Looking back, maybe that's a good thing, because the council would've used that as another strike against me and Gideon.

I could've sought his permission and the special key needed to access the restricted area. However, with the investigation into our relationship, they would twist it and accuse him of favoritism, even though the entire purpose is to help Milo. That would just be a check in the wrong box and set Gideon one step closer to losing his job.

I just can't let that happen.

The Council is watching him too closely.

I could sneak in, but there are magical alarms set to go off without a special key.

Damn. I'm going to have to figure out how to get around that.

However, there is one thing I have yet to try, and that's confront Agatha. She has let this drag out for too long. She can put a stop to this for sure. I just have to make her see reason and understand Milo is more than a pet. He's a brilliant human being with an amazing mind, a knack for alchemy, and has passion for days. He's a living human being.

And she is slowly killing him, whether she realizes it or not.

Surely there is a way to reach her and make her see reason.

Only one way to find out.

It's risky though. My interference on his behalf could set her over the edge, especially if she truly doesn't care about Milo's life. Making matters worse is the last thing I want to do. But I just can't keep standing by and watching him fade away every single day.

I have to do something.

I barely watch where I'm going as I navigate through the numerous halls to House of Drakon's door and realize, I had been so lost in my thoughts of saving Milo, I made it in what seems like record time.

I stare at the door knowing full and well what I'm about to do can either help Milo by appealing to any sense of human decency Agatha may have, or it could result in a devastating spiral toward Milo's end. Making his condition worse is not on the list of things to do. So, I have to at least give the gentle approach a try.

I can't keep debating if I'm helping or hurting. I've got to do *something*. At least by talking to her I can maybe figure out what she's doing to him and why. This could ultimately help save Milo.

Taking a deep breath, I lift my fist… and knock.

CHAPTER FIFTEEN

No one answers.

After taking a steadying breath, I lift my fist and tap my knuckles on the door again. This time, a redheaded student answers the door with her hair piled on top of her head. Wide rimmed glasses sit on the bridge of her nose as her green eyes take in my appearance.

"Can I help you?" she asks as she scratches at one of the numerous freckles that covers her face.

"I'm here to see Agatha. Is she around?"

"I'll go check. Just give me a moment."

I nod. "Sure. Thank you."

"Yup." The door shuts.

The click of the knob being released echoes through the nearly empty hallway. I only wait a few moments before the sound of the knob jiggles and the door opens again. This time, with Agatha standing in an opening barely wide enough for her head to fit through.

Her blue eyes light up as she observes me standing on the other side of the door waiting. "Wren, what a pleasant surprise."

Yeah, right.

I fight the urge to roll my eyes.

She opens the door the rest of the way, her lips curling into a triumphant smile. "Come in."

I stare at her in shock for a few moments. Agatha is actually being rather hospitable, and I step across the threshold. Instantly, I dodge out of the way as a giant, fully-grown harpy eagle lashes out at me with its beak. As I tuck and roll, coming up on my knees I face the creature that almost took my arm off.

Well there goes that moment of believing in her hospitality.

"What the…" I take in the sheer size of just how big the creatures are fully grown, and it's no wonder how Soren knew the one on Crimson Isles was a baby. This thing is massive. He looks like he could easily carry me off and pick my bones clean in thirty seconds flat. But what the hell is he doing in the common room? He should be outside.

Agatha giggles. "Oh my goodness, Herbert! No. Wren here is our guest." She looks to me. "So sorry. Are you okay?"

I'm pretty sure dear, sweet, Herbert could swallow my entire head if he wanted to. Looks like he aims to, the way he opens his beak and stares at me. I look from the giant bird to Agatha and give her a deadly look. She can act like that near miss was a simple mishap all she wants to. I know better than that, and it tells me exactly how the rest of this conversation is going to go.

"I'm fine." I stand from my crouch and smooth out my clothes, not letting the bird or Agatha out of my sight.

She gestures to the bird. "This is Herbert. He's very protective and gets along with everyone in House of Drakon."

Uh-huh.

"Take a seat." She gestures to the couch that Milo and I once shared, and my stomach clenches. It's also awfully close to the harpy eagle and would force me to turn my back to it.

"No, thanks. I won't be here long." Yeah, that attack was far from an accident much less out of protection for Agatha. "Why is he here?" I point to the bird.

She shrugs, her curls bouncing with a slight golden

glow. "Isn't he wonderful? We got permission from my father and the professor of magical creatures to bring him to Blackbriar and study him in class."

"Headmaster Storm allowed him to be chained in this room?" I'm sure she twisted the truth to an unbelievable degree, but I don't buy it one bit that Gideon would allow a creature like this to be chained up in the common room of House of Drakon. There's more to this, and I'm going to use pampered princess's pride against her to find out.

She lifts a finger to her lips. "Shhhh. It's a secret he's in here." She pouts as she approaches the bird who angles his head toward her as she nears. She scratches the feathers at the top of his head. "I just hated seeing him out on the island all by himself and in the cold. He flew right up to the window over there, and I decided that as long as he's quiet, he can stay."

I quirk an eyebrow.

This girl is nuts.

"So, like an idiot, you bring a dangerous creature in here?"

She faces me with a scowl. "What does a half-human from a troll village know about harpy eagles? He's worth more than you."

I feign a hurt expression. But she doesn't know it's for show.

She regains her smug attitude and continues. "The richest mage families pay my father's farm tons of money just to have a harpy eagle. Something you could never understand."

I cross my arms. "If he's worth so much, genius, why did you bring him here? To eat people?"

A dangerous glint in her eye tells me that I've cracked her exterior. "For your information, he is fully trained, unlike that feral." She gasps and clasps her hands together. In her anger, she let something slip that she didn't mean to.

"So… you know about the feral on Crimson Isles. Wouldn't be surprised if it came from your dad's farm. And, infected with the plague too."

"The plague? No, you're lying. You're just jealous because you lost. Milo is mine."

I shake my head and pinch the bridge of my nose. "Speaking of… what have you done to Milo?"

She casually walks in front of the bird and gazes at me, shaking her head as if pitying me. "When I first arrived here, he was the first guy to ever talk to me like I was a normal person. Like I wasn't an heiress to a massive fortune."

She's goading me. Am I supposed to be jealous of her family's wealth? Bitch, please. Still, I follow her with my gaze as she makes her way to where the bird's chain is hooked into the wall.

"He didn't care about kissing my ass because of my father's name or legacy," she gestures to the harpy eagle. "I liked that about him."

She stops and faces me as she runs a dainty finger along the chain. "In fact, I liked *him*."

"Good for you…" I shrug, crossing my arms over my chest. "Why take him from me though? What did you honestly hope to accomplish by twisting his body the way it is?"

She chuckles darkly. "Well, if I want something— or… someone," she smiles. "I get it."

"You're insane and spoiled." I drop my arms to my sides, hands clenching into fists. "Can't you even see what you are doing to him? He's dying! Forgetting things I know he wouldn't and shouldn't. Looking sick and pale, not even going to class. It's ruining him. You're destroying the man I love."

She sighs. "Take a look around you, Wren. We're in a school of magic. What's the point of magic if we can't use it to get what we want?"

"At what cost? Milo's life?" The volume in my voice is rising, and I'm starting to tremble with the growing anger within me. It's getting harder to control myself.

"If you care so much, then promise me you'll give him up. I can take care of him."

"Go to hell."

Agatha shrugs as she takes the chain in her hand and pulls on it ever so slightly, loosening it from the wall. The bird makes a noise and shakes out his neck. The feathers on the top of his head form a crown, and he makes another squawk as he looks at me. Agatha's eyes lift to mine as she smiles, dangerously close to letting the chain go completely.

I lift my head, squaring my shoulders. "Your time with Milo is up. I've tried to talk to you, woman to woman. But it's not working. Threaten me with the damn bird one more time, I'll make sure you don't have hands to control or tame *anything* ever again."

Something red glows from under Agatha's shirt as she glares at me in response to my threat. My magic's ever-fading response to Milo pulls at me. He's getting closer. The sick smile on Agatha's face confirms it.

The necklace has to be the key to all of this. I didn't see it before Milo started acting weird, and it glows as Milo makes his way toward our little conflict.

"Better run along, Wren. You're wearing out your welcome here. Besides, Milo is already on his way to me. I know how to give him what he wants. You may not want to stick around for that."

Damn it all, the idiot actually lets the chain dangle a little more. That move is the last straw with me. I look around the room, wondering where that redhead who answered the door is. Hell, I need anyone to show up right now. Just to witness how incredibly psycho this bitch is. She's got gall, that's for sure. But I'm not going to wait like a damsel. I'm going to make sure she learns just who she is dealing with.

A swirl of magic dances across my fingers like lightning, and I zap her hand with my magic to keep her from loosening the chain. She drops it and backs away, huffing and eyeing me indignantly. She reciprocates with a ball of light aimed straight for my head. I duck, barely in time. The scent of singed hair fills my nostrils, and I count it as yet another reason to kick her ass. This woman is out for my blood, and I'll be damned if she sees a drop of it spilled.

Herbert screeches and tries to lunge for me, despite still being chained up. I stand up straight and punch him in the face with my magic-infused fist. I can feel the moment of impact, connecting with some tissue beneath his feathery face and part of his beak, but my magic helps me absorb the force while delivering damage. The harpy eagle extends his wings and cries out. Apparently, the bird had never suffered a punch before.

I quickly duck and twist, shooting an icy shard toward the tapestry against the wall that's now on fire, thanks to Agatha's ball of light. Dark smoke plumes into the air as my ice spell extinguishes the flames.

Agatha takes advantage of my desire for House of Drakon to not burn down and tries to catch me with another ball of light. She hurls it at me with a ferocity that reveals her utter hatred for me. Too bad it misses me and hits the bird.

Her magic smashes against him and bursts like a firecracker. He groans and teeters before falling over.

I glance at his body and notice he's still breathing.

Ugh.

I cautiously step back as Agatha screams at the top of her lungs.

"Look at what you made me do!" She seethes. "You will pay for that!"

I shake my head. "No, I won't. That was all you, baby girl."

She charges me. But I'm prepared. As soon as she is close enough, I land a roundhouse kick to her stomach. She stumbles backward, eyes wide with the realization that I can easily kick her ass.

She looks to Herbert for help, who is now coming to from the blow she dealt him. She crawls toward the chain on the wall. A dangerous gleam in her eyes tells me that she's going to finally yank it free and let Herbert come for me.

I take my chance to get out of there before I'm harpy eagle dinner.

I slam the door behind me, speeding down the hall and turning corners, my heart pounding in my chest. I finally stop to catch my breath, but only when I'm sure she hasn't followed me.

I'm more determined now than ever to get into that restricted section. That girl won't listen to reason, and she's willing to wager Milo's life on the idea that I'll just walk away because she has wealth and deadly magic. I know for sure it's a curse that Milo is under. And it's about damn time I get into that restricted section and find out which one it is.

Time is running out.

CHAPTER SIXTEEN

In Soren's classroom, I pace the floor in front of his desk as angry flames pulsate along my body. Soren leans back in his seat behind his desk, arms crossed over his chest. Jesse sits perched on a desk near me and he casually observes my pacing. I'm so angry, I can barely think. That fight with Agatha was close. The harpy eagle she controls damn near took my arm off. And I'm sure if I had stayed there a moment longer, Herbert would have taken off my head.

"Are you going to tell us what this is about?" Soren asks as his eyes follow my pacing. There's a hitch of concern in his voice that makes me look at him.

"Agatha," I finally say. I'm not able to give any more information just yet. The name says it all. At least, the name *should* say enough until I can calm down and actually go into further detail. I keep running the whole event through my mind. The audacity of keeping a bloodthirsty bird in the commons room, the controlling and manipulative way she practically dangled me in front of the giant bird.

"Yes, we both understand she's behind your sudden change in mood," he says, almost pensively, "but why? Tell us what happened, Wren."

I glare at Soren. Not because I'm mad at him, but because I am just so freaking angry. He doesn't even flinch. I almost smirk. I'm grateful that he just lets me pace and process as much as I need to until I'm ready to talk. Jesse too. Both of them patiently wait. I keep taking deep breaths to try to help, but the more I think about her and the overgrown pigeon, the angrier I get.

"You're hot. Literally," Jesse says with a devious smirk. "We should ignite her more often."

My pacing is thrown off by that comment as I stop to look at him. He smirks proudly, like he knows he got to me. That was a clever move on his part. I take in my skin, the subtle glow traveling down my arms, and the heat radiating from my forearms. I shake my head, laughing sarcastically under my breath. "I highly recommend you don't. This isn't exactly fun for me."

He shrugs. "Well, I mean you're smoking hot on any given day. But it's nice to see you smiling."

And I truly am. I didn't realize it until he pointed it out to me. Being with them helps me to calm down, if even a little.

I take in a deep, calming breath. The flames along my skin start to die down and my skin radiates with golden magic. "Trust me, I would rather be destroying something right now." I face my two men. "Did you guys know she has a harpy eagle chained up in the commons of Drakon?"

Soren sits forward, anger burning through his eyes. "What." It's not really a question but comes out more like a statement of disbelief. It's flat, and deep.

I nod and hold up two fingers, counting them off as I explain. "First, she invites me in, and I almost lose an arm. Second, she tries to let him loose on me."

Soren shakes his head, standing from his seat and propping himself over the top of his desk. "Something needs to be done about this. There are strict rules in place for the safety and protection of all the students. That eagle should not be anywhere near a common room much less in one." He's seething now, and his skin starts to glow with his fire magic. "I'll take care of it after you finish telling me what else happened?"

I walk to the wall behind his desk and lean against

it. "She not so subtly implied she stole Milo from me because she gets everything she wants and wanted him. She doesn't care about his condition as long as he's her slave. She practically admitted that she is responsible for the whole thing. And all because she's a spoiled brat."

Jesse stands from his perch. "Sounds like this is definitely something Gideon needs to be involved in."

"I agree," Soren says. "But until he can address it, please be careful of the actions you take. He can't protect you with the council watching every single step we take."

"That's not all," I say, holding up my index finger on my right hand. "She's wearing a necklace with a ruby pendant that glows anytime Milo is near. I noticed it when this first started at Lady Alene's party, and again today. The first time she hid it under her shirt when she noticed I saw it, almost like she was scared I would take it from her. But she didn't bother hiding it this time."

"That could hold the answer we are looking for, but unless we can examine it, we won't be able to figure out what the enchantment is or how to reverse it. She probably didn't bother with hiding it now, because she's cocky and she thinks you're jealous of her."

I snort. "Yeah, totally what's going on here."

"I know." Soren holds his hands up in defense. "But it still doesn't change the fact we need to get that necklace to prove it is what's behind Milo's affliction. We need something solid to prove she's responsible. Right now, we have a plausible pendant and your word against hers."

I groan. "What did you want me to do? Snatch the damn thing off her neck?"

"That would be a good start," Jesse adds. "I can set something up." He smiles deviously, eyes alight with a chance to stir up some trouble.

"No." Soren shakes his head. "No rule breaking. We have to keep our noses clean for now."

I sigh. "Look, I know the necklace is the key to it. I know I'm right, and though I can't prove it right this minute, she's responsible. And while we're standing here, Milo is slowly fading away."

"I'll talk to Gideon and see if Milo can be ordered to the infirmary. So long as he remains the headmaster, he still has strings he can pull, and the safety and wellbeing of the students under him are still top priority."

"And then what?" I ask. "He can't go anywhere without Agatha nearby."

"I know. We can ban visitors. Hopefully, this way,

we can keep Agatha away from Milo long enough to run an assessment."

I stand straight. "I want to be there."

Soren shakes his head. "I know you care about him, we all do. But by allowing you in and keeping Agatha out, that could make things worse. If not for you, for Milo. Let me handle this part."

"If it would help, I'd be happy to keep you distracted," Jesse offers. "For however long it takes."

I smile. He's good at distractions, for sure. But I don't think it would work very well. Despite his best efforts, and believe me, they are amazingly delightful efforts, my mind would always make its way back to Milo. And knowing Jesse, he would talk me into breaking a few rules. Right now, we can't afford that. "Thanks, but I probably won't be great company to keep."

He shrugs. "I'll deal."

On second thought, maybe the break is exactly what I need. I've been so consumed with trying to find a way to help Milo, I've neglected Jesse, and that is inexcusable. Besides, when Milo goes to the infirmary, I won't be allowed in. "Okay. You asked for it, though."

He chuckles. "Challenge accepted."

I smile and turn my attention to Soren. "What's wrong with Milo is not a typical spell. I've done enough research to know that. It doesn't appear like any curse I can find information on either—at least not without traversing the restricted area."

He nods. "I'll see what I can do about that. Any other updates?"

Jesse approaches Soren's desk. "I haven't been able to gather anything we can use. The girl is surprisingly clever and hard to track."

"Clever" is one word I wouldn't use to describe that girl.

"She's not working alone," I say. "So, we need to find out who's helping her."

Soren's brow furrows. "True. No one at her skill level should be able to do anything like this. Keep your eyes and ears open, Wren. We'll figure this out and help Milo come back to us."

I nod as my heart aches for him. I wish I could just blow the girl up, but all that would do is cause more trouble for me and my team. It does warm my heart though to know my men are trying as hard as I am to get Milo back to us. He's their brother in arms. An attack on one is an attack on them all.

"What about Savannah? Has she reported?" Jesse asks.

Soren shakes his head. "She's still working on it. I told her to switch gears and see if she can figure out the information we need without going directly to Agatha herself. She also reported that Agatha has sometimes gone to the kitchens at odd hours, but not why."

"I know," I say. "Meeting with the cook."

Soren's expression becomes a mix of anger and confusion.

"The day Savannah and I went to the spa, I stopped at the kitchens to grab a quick bite. Caseus mentioned something about being up so early but when he turned and saw me, it was like he wasn't expecting me to be standing there. He was counting on someone else. My money is on Agatha and the cook being up to something. I think he's the one that has been helping her."

"That's a plot twist," Jesse muses. "Sounds like there's more mischief to be had."

"But it sounds like Savannah is keeping a safe distance as promised." I sigh with relief.

"Yes," Soren says. "We're all doing what we can to get to the bottom of this."

"And what about granting me access to the restricted area in the library?" I ask as frustration once again takes ahold of me. "I need to get inside there."

"Hold tight."

I cross my arms. "If it comes down to it, I *will* sneak in."

Soren grimaces. "If you can wait, I swear I'll have an answer by tomorrow. Remember, you're being watched."

I reluctantly nod. "I'm so going to ring the necks of every single Order member I come across. My personal thank you for attempting to break my team up."

"Until then, stay out of trouble." Soren levels his gaze on mine. "I need to go report the creature in the Drakon commons to Gideon. He'll know what to do."

I huff. "Fine."

"Now, now, Wren. There are other ways to have fun." Jesse walks up to me and slides an arm around my waist. He salutes Soren and escorts me toward the door. Once out of ear shot, he whispers, "Want to do some mischief?"

I smile darkly. "I thought you would never ask."

CHAPTER SEVENTEEN

Frantic knocking on my bedroom door wakes me in the middle of the night. I peel my eyes open and search my dark room. Moonlight shines through the window at my left, casting enough light to see that everything is in order. My intuition isn't spiking, and I don't feel the incredible weight of being watched, like I had earlier in the year. For all intents and purposes, everything is quite peaceful.

I wonder if I had mistakenly heard the sound, chalking it up to a figment of my imagination. Lying back down, I get comfortable, pulling my comforter up to my chin and snuggling into my pillow. As soon as I close my eyes, the knocking happens once more.

I groan and pull myself from my comfy bed to answer the door. I guess it wasn't my imagination. As I walk to the door, I seriously consider punching the person on the other side. I was actually having very pleasant dreams. But I also know that if someone is rapping on my door this early in the morning, it has to be important.

Once I twist the knob, the door opens. Soren shoves his way inside and I close the door. "Please, come in."

"Get dressed," he says, urgency filling his voice as he fumbles through my closet. "We have to go."

This wakes me up instantly. "What's going on?" I slip out of my pajamas and quickly slide on the jeans and t-shirt Soren tossed onto my bed.

"We can't talk here. Just hurry."

Normally, I would demand an answer, but considering the timing of him showing up at my door and the urgency in his voice, I don't argue. Instead, I nod and quickly toss on my socks and shoes and slip into my leather jacket before following Soren out my door.

As we make our way through the halls of the silent castle and out toward the garden, my mind runs wild with the possible reasons why I would be woken up in the middle of the night and dragged out into the frigid island temperatures.

It could be Milo, struggling for life in the infirmary as tubes and hoses cover his body, and I'm needed to say goodbye. That thought alone nearly makes me falter in my steps. Soren looks over his shoulder at me, concern etched in his expression. I nod at him to let him know I'm okay. He looks forward again without question.

The reason could also have something to do with Gideon. He may be arrested, hauled off in chains because of our forbidden love. I gulp and grip my chest as pain stabs me like an invisible knife to the heart.

The reasons could literally be anything, whether it be Savannah losing her dad to the plague, the Order capturing my father again after his disguise somehow faded in front of the wrong people, or there could be another possible reason that I can't fathom at the moment.

Whatever it is, it's not good. That's all I know, and I can't let myself get wrapped up in emotions without first knowing the facts. I force myself to take a few deep breaths as I continue to follow Soren's hasty steps.

I now realize where we are heading, and that doesn't lessen the feeling of a cold lump in my stomach. I can only think of the worst of the previous scenarios. Somehow, the icy chill in the air breaks through my core and though I pull my leather jacket tighter around me, it doesn't do much good. Once we reach our secret meeting spot, the illusion is already in place, with Jesse, Lady Alene, and Savannah already here.

Gideon joins us soon after, and my mind instantly snaps to Milo. I start to believe something horrible has happened to him, but I don't want to even think about or accept that thought.

This meeting is about Milo. And I don't want to breathe.

"Wren," Gideon says as he pulls me into him. I cling to him because this is going wrong so quickly, and I just can't even fathom what he's about to say next. I don't want to hear the words. I don't want to even think them.

"What's going on?" I hear myself ask. I'm running on autopilot at this moment. It's surreal. Almost as if I'm watching the things unfold in first-person and being absolutely powerless to stop it.

"The council has finished their investigation." Gideon's words come at me with a rush of relief but at the same time, a brand new dread breaks through and my head is spinning.

I pull away from him to take in his handsome face, gleaning any clues from his expression. His mesmerizing gaze takes hold of mine and I almost become lost within them. A slight crease between his eyebrows grabs my attention, and that tells me all I need to know.

This isn't about Milo. But this meeting isn't full of good news either. It's about him.

"You lost your job?" Even though I don't intend for it to, it sounds like a question. This is it. I'm losing Gideon for sure now. It's not fair, and I don't know what I'm going to do without him. How are we going to save Milo if he's not here?

He nods once, pulling me into him. "It's not your fault."

Yes, it is. If I hadn't nearly been captured by my aunt, and Gideon jumping to my aid, she would have never caught on to more than she should have, and this entire mess would all be avoided. As much as it is comforting that he doesn't blame me, I harbor enough blame for the both of us.

"What are you going to do now?" I cling to him again. I don't know what's going to happen from here on out, and I want to take in as much of him as I can.

"I have to leave in a few hours. I'll stay in contact with Soren and try to help as much as I can, but my hands are tied. At some point, you'll be able to visit me at my estate."

Well, at least we still have that.

It still feels like he's being ripped from me. Now three of the most important men of my life aren't going to be around. I'll be separated from Gideon, my father, and Milo. Even though I may get to see Milo, I can't interact with him. And that breaks my heart just as badly as if he's physically away from me. He's being kept at a distance. And now, so is Gideon, by being removed completely from Blackbriar.

I know that the Order is behind this and they want to make me vulnerable. They failed to capture me, and they failed to steal the meteorite I merged with, if that's even possible. Now it seems this new line of attack is working. This is all distressing, for sure, but I refuse to give them the satisfaction of thinking they've won.

"A formal announcement will be made before classes," Gideon continues. "I just wanted to give you a heads-up, so you weren't blindsided by it."

"I appreciate that," I say, pulling away. I face the rest of the group. My friends, my team, my family.

"I will be here to help you in any way I can," Lady Alene says.

I smile and reach for her stony hand. "Thank you."

As soon as my fingers brush hers, my magic, deep within my core, shudders within me with a vibrating warmth I've never felt before. An odd vision of Lady

Alene flashes in front of me. But the Alene in my vision is made of flesh, and she lies peacefully asleep, arms crossed over her chest, and her right hand clasping a small silver box.

I gasp, breaking contact and peering into the eyes of the current Alene, whose stony façade encases the soul of our Patron Mage.

"Did you do that?" I ask her.

The men look at us in bewilderment, while Savannah gives me a knowing look. Lady Alene never takes her eyes off me. "You saw something?"

I shake my head, wondering if I've seen too many depictions of Alene's life from the celebrations. Maybe I'm finally cracking. "I'm just tired. I've been so worried about Milo, and now they're firing Gideon."

Lady Alene's lips part, as if she's ready to tell me something, but she falters and falls silent.

"You still have me here, and Soren." Jesse still looks a little confused at what just happened, but he gently cups my shoulder, as if saying that though he doesn't understand, he will always be there for me. I lean into him, grateful for the gesture.

"I may not be able to show you my affection as often as I would like, but I refuse to remove myself completely," Soren says as fire burns through my veins.

Having my men comfort me like this, it feels amazing. I adore them for their devotion to me. With their support, I feel capable. I know we will get through this.

"Now that you have been warned," Gideon says, getting down to business, "it's time we move to the next point to cover—the Order."

"Assholes," I mutter. They're behind all this mess. I know it deep in my gut. My intuition has never been wrong before, and I have little reason to doubt it now.

"Fair assessment," Jesse adds.

"Be that as it may, that's not the point I was going to make," Gideon says. "I'm afraid the harpy eagle Agatha Collins chained up in the commons of Drakon isn't the only one on the island."

"What? Are you kidding?" Savannah's furious expression mirrors my own. She practically took the words out of my mouth.

I ball my fists, remembering how I nearly lost an arm to Agatha's ferocious pet. "Why are they here? Especially after what happened on Crimson Isles?"

Gideon shakes his head. "It's *because* of what happened there that the other harpy eagles are here. Their handler, Demitri Collins, is a rich alumnus who has pull with the new headmaster. He claims that since this island is a known haven for magical creatures, that the harpy eagles unaffected by the plague would be safer here. He finally admitted that the feral escaped his farm and he needs to quarantine. Unfortunately, there are wealthy and powerful mage families backing him, knowing that they need the farms to keep the harpy population in check."

I don't need an explanation on who this Demitri guy is. Like father, like daughter. "So, Agatha's father paid the new headmaster off?"

"Not necessarily, but maybe," Gideon says. "The change in headmaster has been in the works for quite some time. It seems they had already concluded how my investigation would end. Members of the council had say in this matter with the harpies. As such, I'm stripped of any authority."

"Well, this is wonderful," Jesse says. "How do we even know the big birds they're bringing to the island are completely free of the plague? I've got to admit, now I'm almost looking fondly on the pranks my brothers pull. I'd rather face those little demons than an island of infected, man-eating birds. I'm too pretty to eat."

Jesse actually has a point. Well, about the birds anyway. There's no telling what would happen if an infected harpy eagle manages to get here. The effects could be devastating.

OLIVIA ASH

I let out a slow breath. "Guys, if even one of the harpies here is infected, that would cause total chaos. It will put everyone in danger."

"But aren't the ones from the farm all trained?" Savannah asks. "They wouldn't attack unless provoked, would they?"

Soren shakes his head. "It won't matter if they go rabid in response to the disease. Part of the lab results I received from the magusari indicated a link between the infection and the creature's behavior."

"It's all too convenient for everything to happen like this," I mutter. Any obstacle that prevented the Order from reaching and cornering me—they're knocking down. And as much as I hate to admit it, their methods are working. They've successfully removed two of my men. Agatha's deal with Milo is most definitely part of the Order's plan. My father forced into hiding, living in disguise due to their unverified allegations, and now Gideon, because my aunt let slip that our relationship was more than what one should be between a headmaster and his student.

Well, I've got news for them. They're about to learn that I don't go down that easily.

"I'm sorry to add onto our pile of problems," Savannah steps forward, "but I wanted to update you all about Milo and Agatha. I tried to do some digging into Agatha's past for anything of note. Something is actively blocking me from my visions."

A pinch forms in the center of my forehead. "Of course. Powerful cloaking and dark magic with this girl? This has Order written all over it."

As selfish and entitled as Agatha is, she doesn't strike me as an evil mastermind. Someone in the Order is helping her. Guiding her. But I don't give a damn if she's a willing participant or a foolish pawn. All I care about is saving Milo.

"It would support my own suspicions as well," Gideon adds.

"You always thought there were Order members here, but you couldn't be sure. Deacon Lawrence made a misstep during Wren's trials and we all know how that ended. I remember you said that you would keep an eye on the those you couldn't read well," Soren points out. "It's all making sense. They were probably under our noses this entire time."

"And we just didn't have enough information to connect the dots," Gideon finishes.

"First thing we need to do is get Milo back. That's step one. If we can save him, he can likely bridge the gap in understanding. Maybe even tell us who else, besides Caseus, Agatha has been in contact with," Soren adds.

Speaking of contact and help, I turn my thoughts toward the woman who I believe could help us with Milo's malady. "I could try talking to Professor Crosswell again, but she's busy trying to find a cure for the plague," I say.

Savannah beams and clasps her hands together. "Thank goodness. I hope she finds it soon."

I'd feel like such a jerk if I tried to pull Professor Crosswell away from finding a cure that could save thousands and protect my best friend's dad and brothers. I need to come up with another option. "The necklace has something to do with all of this. I need access to the restricted section of the library, which has yet to be approved." I level my gaze on Gideon. He shrugs. "Now it's looking like I won't get that access with you leaving."

"Something tells me your new headmaster won't grant you access," he says. "Not without coming clean about your intentions, and that's not something I'd recommend sharing."

"I was trying to hold off because of the investigation, but since that's over, there's no more need to play nice."

Looks like I'm going to have to break in. How hard could that be?

Gideon eyes me, as if discerning exactly what I'm

thinking. He crosses his arms over his chest and falls silent, but his eyes shift out of focus and I can tell he's piecing things together as well. "I'll do what I can from my estate. Now that I will be off the island, I won't have to be as careful. I can reach out to my contacts and see if they know of anything. I'll talk to Lionel and Michael and see if they know of a spell that relates to Milo's condition."

My shoulders fall with that. I hate the idea that my father is being dragged into this because his assumed identity is the only thing keeping him off the Order's radar. I really would rather he stop risking blowing his cover. He's been through enough. But I also know my father better than to think he will sit this out. My father is cunning and resourceful. I'm sure he would be an immense help.

"Whatever we find, we need to do it fast. Milo's condition is deteriorating by the day," I say. I bite the corner of my lower lip and shove down my worry and heartache for him. Only a level, logical mind is going to be the best help. I can't get stuck in emotions now.

"Agreed," Gideon says.

"One last thing," Soren says. "From now on, if there needs to be a group talk, act up in my class. That will give me the signal. I'll delve out detention and we can have a discussion then."

Gideon sighs. "I'm afraid we are out of time." He settles his gaze on me and half-heartedly smiles. "I'll see you soon. I promise."

"I'm holding you to that promise," I say.

And he knows I will.

CHAPTER EIGHTEEN

H ours later, everyone is gathering in the arena to be introduced to the new headmaster. Loud murmurs fill the air as people vocally voice their displeasure with Gideon's removal. They apparently don't know the reason why, and I'm not inclined to give them the answer.

Part of me is extremely grateful they don't know the ins and outs on why Gideon is no longer headmaster. I sincerely hope they don't find out. If they do, that could spell a whole lot of trouble for me here, and I refuse to let a single soul stand in the way of my happiness. This is my home. I refuse to see this as a prison. Ever.

The room is virtually bare from any decorations

except for Blackbriar's tapestry hanging proudly from the vast ceiling above us. A large podium sits at the far wall, taking up the center. That's probably where the announcement will be made. Tables and chairs fill the room, and it looks like we're going to be forced to sit with our own houses during the introduction.

I wonder what sort of headmaster the next one will be, or if there will be any explanation into why there is a new one. I hope there's not a horribly detailed list of Gideon's supposed misdeeds. He's an honorable man who I couldn't help but fall in love with, and he with me. I hope that if any reason is given, it's just something to the effect of there being circumstances that required a new headmaster, and though Gideon is no longer on the island, he sends his best wishes. Something that keeps his good name from being marred.

Jesse joins my side. I know it's him judging by the reaction of my magic. It's soothing to have him here. My nerves are a mess and I'm worried about not only Milo, but Gideon as well. But with Jesse's cool magic flowing through me, I feel more at ease, and I'm grateful he's here with me.

Savannah eventually weaves her way through the crowd of students to join us. I observe her nodding casually to some students and smiling at others, as she makes her way in our direction. She approaches my side simply nodding in greeting and stands next to me.

"How are you holding up?" she asks as she slightly leans into me so that I can hear her over the dull roar of the crowded arena.

I shrug. "As well as can be expected."

After all, Gideon has been removed from his rightful place at this school, and though he insists I'm not to blame for this, I feel responsible. Whatever happens, I'm going to clear his name so he can reclaim his position. He loved his job and it tears me up that I'm the reason why he had to leave.

She smiles softly and turns her attention to the overfilled room. "Wow, there are a lot of us here."

"Too many, if you ask me," Jesse mutters.

"Not a fan of crowds, Jesse?" I ask, teasing him. I poke his side and smile. He returns the gesture and puts his arm around my shoulder.

"I'm not a fan of all this formality for a new head-master," he says into my ear and I completely understand where he's coming from.

Faculty members appear at the head of the room and a man steps forward and takes the podium. He's tall, handsome, and a coating of salt and pepper fuzz covers his chin in a well-groomed beard. He smiles over the crowd as he takes a stand at the podium. My attention is claimed by Soren, who looks none too happy with things. He frowns as he stares daggers at the back of the man standing at the podium. I don't blame him. His friend, more like a brother, has been ousted. And at a time when we needed him most. Soren's arms are crossed over his chest, and he seems to be the only one standing defensively. All the other faculty members seem to be pretty excited about this man.

"If everyone would please take a seat with their own houses, we'll be starting momentarily." The man's voice is gentle, deep, and charming. It's hard not to want to like him, but if Soren has an issue with this man, I probably want to remain cautious until I learn why. He leaves the podium and joins the line of other faculty members, chatting and smiling, winning over their hearts.

I have a feeling this is our new headmaster. That's what my gut is telling me.

"Welp, catch up with you later," Savannah says as she squeezes the top of my right arm.

"See you." I nod and face Jesse.

He and I share a look. It's the kind that states we are both less than thrilled to be here. He winks before walking away. I let out a breath, shaking my head at the fact that he can be so relaxed at a moment like this. Honestly, it shouldn't surprise me by now.

I turn myself around and join my fellow Phoenix housemates, taking a seat in a corner. So far, it seems like no one is aware of me being behind Gideon's dismissal. One of my housemates, I never caught her name, leans in and asks, "Do you know why Headmaster Storm was dismissed?"

I shrug and shake my head. "No, why?" I lie.

She frowns. "I thought you guys were close or something. Like he was grooming you to take over his spot one day."

A short burst of panic shoots through me. Maybe we weren't as careful as we thought we were being. I clear my throat and sit straighter. "He was training me to hone my magic better, but it was only tutoring. That's all."

"Ah. Okay." She genuinely smiles. "Good to know."

If you say so.

I smile back, but mine is fake.

The murmurs continue to rise in volume. People are pointing and talking about who the new face is standing in a line with the rest of the faculty behind the podium. The man who told us to take a seat with our houses. They all suspect he is the new headmaster as well, and some of the girls sigh wistfully. I hear mutters of how hot and charming he is.

I want to gag.

I catch sight of Jesse and Savannah sitting on opposite sides of the room. They are both focused on the podium at the front of the room. Neither of them is talking with their housemates. Their expressions are relatively blank. Jesse turns his gaze toward me and smirks. I smile in return.

Finally, the announcement.

The same person who took the podium before stands behind it once again. "Thank you all kindly for showing up." He smiles, despite a few boos and hisses. I can't help but smirk. Seems like not everyone is in favor of this new guy. Makes me proud to know that Gideon had made such a good impression on the students here. For now, it seems like only us third-years and fourth-years remain suspicious of him.

I look at Jesse, smirking to himself as I stifle a giggle of my own.

The speaker scans the room, eyes bright and sharp, yet retains a calm expression. He's not even fazed by the students clamoring for Gideon's return. It almost seems to make him try harder.

"My name is Travis Westbrook," his voice booms throughout the arena, causing the voices of dissent to quiet down. His piercing gaze demands attention. "It is my honor to assume the position of interim headmaster."

The lined-up faculty applaud him—except Soren—and mostly first-year students join in. The students who've been here the longest, while no longer shouting Gideon's name, display their displeasure by remaining silent and placing their hands in their laps.

Westbrook doesn't seem to mind. In fact, he grins as if someone had just given him a compliment. "I actually taught here many years ago. And so, I am certainly no stranger to Blackbriar. In fact," he leans into the podium, "they used to say I was here when the castle was first built!"

Despite themselves, the third and fourth-years rumble with laughter, joining in with the already won over crowd.

Hell, even I caught myself smirking, before I remember he took Gideon's job.

"Though I cannot disclose the reasons for my being here, I can assure you that I will do my best to live up to the great name of my predecessor."

More applause. Even more students are joining in and buying into his charm. I roll my eyes.

He pauses, waiting for the noise to die down. "I can never be as amazing as the great Mr. Storm, but what I

OLIVIA ASH

can do is help lead the school with strength and integrity, for as long as you'll let me. Do we have a deal?"

A series of applause roars through the room.

This man is a real crowd pleaser.

Soren shakes his head, crossing his arms over his chest. The rest of the faculty seem rather impressed by him, joining in with the applause. I'll have to pull him aside to figure out what it is about this new headmaster that rubs him the wrong way. Whenever that will be. I'm sure whoever this man is, he's here for more than just assuming the role of headmaster until Gideon can return. I'm sure there is a number of bullet points under his hidden agenda that he's going to want to check off.

My suspicions are rising. The Order wouldn't throw out Gideon only to replace him with a charming former teacher. I'm not so willing to credit him as being anywhere near Gideon's character and stature. My intuition tells me there is more to this man than meets the eye, and for as long as it takes until Gideon can take his seat back, I'll remain cautious and as distant as possible.

I check for Jesse and Savannah's reaction as well. They sit back in their seats. Jesse has his hands behind his head, casually observing the crowd around him and listening to the new headmaster's speech. Savannah sits with her hands folded in front of her, resting on the table.

Once this circus is all over, I'll meet up with them and have a chat about their impressions of our new headmaster. I suspect they will be similar to my own.

"Now, a little about myself," Headmaster Westbrook says. "I'm a southern Georgia boy, born and raised. My family originates from Ireland, where we come from a proud, long line of mages."

This man must love to smile and hear himself talk. He doesn't sound southern. Not in the way that Savannah does. He also seems to play heavily on his charm, which is another red checkmark in my book of warnings.

While he continues to regale everyone with his rags to riches story, which I'm sure is completely fascinating, I have no desire to listen to it any longer. I rake my gaze along the crowd captivated by the speech our new headmaster is giving and notice not a single person is going to notice me slipping out.

With a smirk, I take my leave.

With the halls completely empty and everyone sitting in the arena, ensnared by the new headmaster's speech, I move easily and quickly through the halls to

OLIVIA ASH

my room. I have to get into that restricted section to find any information I can to help Milo.

Once I'm in my room, I'm caught by the sight of a small package on the foot of my bed and a letter resting on top of them. I look around for anything out of place. I'm not used to walking into my room and finding things on my bed. I'm immediately suspicious, thinking this is another one of Agatha's tactics to try and get back at me from our little tiff in the Drakon commons.

But upon further inspection, there's no enchantment glowing from them that strikes me as harmful. There's an enchantment for sure, but it's light, soft, and familiar. I pick up the edge of the letter with my index finger and slowly open it.

I instantly recognize the writing and breathe a sigh of relief.

My dearest little bird,

I hear you're having some troubles accessing some hard to reach places. I hope these help. Use them wisely.

Stay safe. Let me know how they work when you can.

See you soon.

I toss the letter to the bed and instantly shred the

200

plain white paper tied with a thin rope to find a pair of gloves.

"Yes!" I do a little dance next to my bed knowing exactly what these gloves are used for.

I'm so going to give my father a huge kiss when I see him.

Examining the gloves, they look like something I would normally wear in the cold weather. They are leather, dyed a dark silver color with a band covering the wrist and an aqua marine charm in the center of the band. Completely unsuspecting.

They are beautiful.

I slip them on for size and they magically stretch to fit my hands perfectly.

"Amazing," I hear myself say.

I pull them off and sit at the foot of my bed. Now it's time to plan. Tomorrow evening, once everyone is in bed, I'll sneak out, and make my way to the library. Though everything in me burns to go now, I have to make every single move carefully. It will be easier to give the academy some time to settle from the excitement of our new, charming headmaster. Besides, I don't know how closely I'm still being watched.

With these gloves, I'll pass through the restricted section without setting off an alarm. It still won't be easy, but now with these gloves, I'm one step closer to finding what I need. Because I'm sure what I need is behind that door.

I tuck the gloves under the mattress at the head of my bed where they will be safe and sound until tomorrow evening. Once the castle is dark and quiet, I'll get what I need. Hopefully without being caught.

Because even though getting into the restricted section just got easier, there is still a lot that can go wrong.

CHAPTER NINETEEN

It feels like huge chunks of me are missing. Though Milo sits feet away from me in class today, I barely feel my magic's response to him. Even less than before.

My initial trip toward the restricted section had me headed off by Caseus, one of the cooks. I couldn't stand the idea of waiting and decided to go last night. Needless to say, it didn't work out as well as I had hoped.

"What are you doing up so late, girl? And at this hour, about in the halls?" the cook had asked when I ran into him.

Students aren't supposed to be out after lights out. So, I had to make up an excuse. "I'm not feeling well.

Heading to the kitchen to fix myself something to settle my stomach."

"I have just the thing for you," he had told me in a creepy way.

"It's quite all right. Don't trouble yourself. I can do it on my own," I said. "Besides, I'll head to my room after that."

"There's always the infirmary, if you're that sick," he muttered, shaking his head and narrowing his eyes on me.

I nodded in agreement, walking around him. "Great idea. I'll head there now."

I didn't go there last night, of course.

I took the long way around the castle, back to the House of Phoenix. I couldn't risk going again that night and resolved to give it another try tonight. Even though I know Milo is withering away more and more and with time running out before the inevitable happens, I have to be extremely cautious about sneaking out again.

This time, I have a new approach.

But now, as I take in the sight of Milo, I have to do something more immediate and purposefully let a few loose papers fall from my notebook. I bend down and scoot over, and whisper to him. "Do you want to go to the infirmary? I can take you."

He barely looks at me. His jaw tightens with anger.

He's upset because right before Gideon left, he tried ordering Milo to the infirmary. He's fighting tooth and nail to stay out of there, so he actually showed up to class today to prove he's able to. But he looks like a zombie.

It used to be that whenever I would get near him, my magic would rush with a cool, almost icy sensation. Emotions ran free with him. I could drop my guard and just be me, without worrying about ridicule. He pushes me to learn more.

Even now.

I want to learn what's gotten a hold of him so I can unchain him. I want to learn how to return him back to his old self. The gentle touch of coolness that fades in and out, lessening as time wears on, really bothers me to no end. Because it's a symbol of Milo himself fading too.

That's just something I absolutely can't let happen.

And now that Gideon is gone and being kept from me too, it's hard. Though he's not completely shut off from me, which is a huge blessing, he's not on the island anymore, and the time we have available to spend together is few and far between. I had become used to his constant presence. To him always being here when I needed him. I lived for those precious moments stolen away in secret where we would share in a kiss. Where it felt like he could really see me. To his magic strengthening mine, making me feel simply *untouchable*.

With him, my magic buzzes stronger than ever.

Now that he's gone, I have to rely on my own devices. With him gone, I won't get an approval for the library. Our new headmaster has won practically the whole island over, except for me and my team. But I have one thing no one knows about, and that's the gloves. I won't need permission. And I won't wait any longer.

After class, I return to my room and finish preparing for my library break in. It's too risky to talk to Headmaster Westbrook. I don't trust anyone put into a place of power by the hand of the Order.

When nightfall hits, I steal through the castle toward the library. I can't wait any longer. Milo can't wait any longer.

I have to do this.

Is it breaking the rules? Yes. Do I risk expulsion from Blackbriar? Absolutely. But doing this to save one of the men I love is worth the risk. I can't just watch Milo wither away and die anymore.

Before, I had my men to worry about. I had to think of the repercussions not only for myself, but them as well. And with the investigation into Gideon, I couldn't risk his position further by acting out on my own. Now that it's over and they've thrown him out, there's no reason for me to hold off.

With Milo's life hanging by a thread, I have to do something.

I've waited for a response for access into the restricted section of the library for months, resorting to digging through every book I could possibly find, and now that I've run out of options, this is the only one left.

I'll deal with the consequences later. For now, Milo needs me.

Under the cover of night, when the rest of the island is sleeping, I float through the halls, silent as a ghost. At each turn, I'm on the lookout for anyone or anything that could make my trip that much harder. Since Headmaster Westbrook with his impeccable charm re-instituted an earlier-than-usual curfew, anyone observing a student sneaking through the halls in the middle of the night is automatic cause for suspicion, and they will likely report me to the headmaster immediately.

I thought about bringing Jesse with me, but the less people involved the better. He has a lot riding on his success here, and I don't want to take that from him, nor ask him to give that up. Savannah too.

Soren? After what just happened with Gideon, it's probably best not to get caught sneaking through the halls at night with a female student. Plus, he would never approve of me breaking into the library, seeing it as too big of a risk.

I have to do this one on my own.

When I finally make it to the library, I pause to calm my breath and ease the nervousness in my hands. After all, I'm well aware of the fact that this could either be a huge success or an epic fail. I slip on my gloves, delighting in the way they feel like they were made for my hands. A smile pulls on my face, and I know this is the right thing to do.

After double checking that no one is in the halls, I dash to the door, place my gloved hand on the handle, and it clicks open. The sound causes me to hold my breath, but I don't waste time pushing the door open and stepping inside. Once the door clicks shut, I release the breath I was holding and turn to face the enormous library with towering shelves filled with books. Practically everything someone needs to know regarding magic is in this room. What's not covered, is hidden behind the door at the back of the library.

The restricted section.

I make my way through the darkened library, dodging chairs and tables. Moonlight is cast through the windows, beaming in muted light, providing just enough for me to see by.

Finally, when I make it to the restricted section, I pause at the door. There are rumors of this door being enchanted in addition to the fact it requires a special key to get in. Alarms will alert the castle to a student breaking in.

I pause to take a breath. Now is the moment of truth. I reach into my power, knowing that if I use too much or too little, regardless of the type of magic I use to unlock the handle, the alarms will go off. I will be forced to yet again come back at a later time, provided I don't get caught. If the alarm is tripped, there is a very real possibility that there will be even more enchantments used on this door to prevent unauthorized access.

Failing is not an option.

Using my magic, I feel for the enchantment on the door. It has a strong vibration, with a sensation of pins and needles. I have to use my magic, and match the vibration, so that when the lock disengages, it doesn't trigger the alarms.

It's a painstaking, agonizing moment that requires an intense level of concentration and precise tweaking of my magic. One wrong move can go horribly wrong.

I focus, taking deep breaths until I feel my power pulsing at the same level. Pins and needles cover my skin, and I know I've reached the right frequency.

I let out a slow breath and place my gloved hand on the handle. The lock clicks, and the knob turns freely.

I'm finally in, but now the real work begins.

Knowing I don't have much time, I quickly move through the large room, searching for the book that I need. It has to be an archaic book of spells and curses, since nothing else in the main library covers the exact thing I need.

So far, it's a whole lot of nothing, as I browse through a few books and make my way to the more disused section. The bookshelves are coated with thick dust. All except for one with a glaring difference. A book is missing from the middle shelf. I try to read the spines on either side of it, but it's no use. It's too dark, and the books are too old and dusty.

I let out a frustrated sigh and continue on. I reach the far wall and turn to the left. A sound catches my attention. It's the door to the room I'm standing in. I hear the click of a lock and I quickly find a dark corner to hide in.

Caseus, the cook, stumbles in, fumbling in the

dark, carrying a stack of books. He slips each one into their rightful place on the shelves. Who in their right mind would give the cook access to the restricted section? It doesn't make sense. Faint light glitters on something strapped to his waist, and I notice it's a key. I'm betting it's either stolen or a counterfeit.

Watching carefully, I make note of where he places all the books. He sticks the last one in the most unusual of places. Not on a shelf with the others, but tucked behind a stack of books in the far corner of the room. With the rest of the books that are marked as damaged and in need of some sort of repair or no longer able to be checked out.

Caseus probably left it there thinking no student would ever access it, and believing he is alone. He doesn't know he's being watched, as I crouch just feet from him. I've already pulled up an illusion that I learned from Jesses recently, to make it seem the spot I'm occupying is just another stack of books. I hold my breath as he approaches my direction, attention alerted to something I don't hear or see.

"Someone there?" he asks.

His eyes narrow on my location, and I feed more energy into the illusion.

He takes another step toward me, and I pray to anyone out there listening that he just gives up and leaves. One more step and he could easily lift his hand and touch me, catching me in the act, creating a lot of hell that I don't need to pay for right now.

Thankfully, he grunts and turns around.

"Caseus, you need a vacation," he grumbles to himself and leaves the restricted section. The click of the lock on the doorknob signals that he's gone and it's safe to come out again.

Without missing a beat, I walk straight to the book he tucked away in the corner with the other disused books in dire need of repair. As I go to touch the book, it zaps me. Shaking out my fingers, I grip the book firmly and open the cover and scan the first few pages.

It's full of dangerous curses. Most of them much more deadly than the one Milo has been put under, but I know, deep in my gut, that this has to be the book.

This is it.

This is the book. I know it.

My heart flutters with excitement as I take the book in my hand, finally having the first solid clue to a way to lift the curse Milo is under.

But time is ticking, and my visit here is running short. I'm going to need Gideon on this with me if I'm going to be able to find the curse and break it. He needs to know what Caseus is up to as well. This will confirm he is working with Agatha.

Tucking the book under my shirt and the waistband of my skirt, I quickly dash out of the library and into the halls, back to my room.

CHAPTER TWENTY

The next evening, I'm sitting in Gideon's kitchen as he pours two cups of coffee. I told him this was going to be a long night, and he felt it was called for. He mixes in a few herbs to prevent a crash after the caffeine wears off and takes a seat across from me.

"So, what have you got for me?" Gideon asks. He holds the rim of his cup to his lips, blows into the hot liquid a couple of times, and then takes a sip.

I pull out my mysterious find and set it on the table.

His eyebrows draw together as he sets his cup on the table and takes the book into his hand. It zaps him too, which makes him jerk a little. He examines the book, running his fingers over the cover and the back, and finally the spine.

215

There's no title on the book, no decoration. It simply looks like an old journal, except that the low hum of magical energy surrounding it indicates it has some strange enchantment on it.

"It's definitely enchanted," he says as though reading my mind. "Old too."

"How can you tell?" I ask, finally taking my mug into my hand. I slip my fingers through the handle and let the warmth fill my fingers, pushing back the cold that seems to surround my body.

"The binding," he says simply.

He flips open the book and thumbs through the pages. He pauses on some of the notes, and as he continues to dig deeper into the script, his frown deepens. "Why was it hidden the way it was? It seems like it was placed there purposefully."

"I watched the cook, Caseus do it. He wanted to make sure it wouldn't be found, but he didn't know I was there, hiding in the shadows watching him."

"Perhaps," Gideon says. "I don't recognize this book. It's definitely archaic with spells that are now illegal, so this is a good place to start."

I smile. "You think so? I was really hoping this would be the book."

"It's a good find, and it very well may be."

"I was going to lead with the pulsating crystal on

Agatha's neck. I truly feel like that is the source of what is afflicting Milo."

Gideon flips through the book and settles on a section noted "*Corpus Et Animam Meum.*" He points at the title. "I think this would be the place to find something like that. Remind me, again, what Milo's symptoms are."

I do so, and with each one, he checks off the list. A perfect match. This is the curse we were looking for, the one we needed to put a name to. We found it. And now, that means we can finally break it.

He hands the book back to me and I take a corner of a napkin and mark the page, sliding it back into my bag. Once I'm done, I sigh, falling into my thoughts about the strength slipping away from Milo and wondering if I'll be able to save him in time. Or if I'm going to be too late.

"The most competent person who understands how to undo the curse and help Milo is Professor Crosswell."

I frown. "She's been a whole lot of help so far."

"She's been trying to work on a cure for the plague," Gideon gently reminds me.

"I know." I sigh. "Fine. I'll take the book to her. And I haven't forgotten about Agatha's necklace. That's what she's using to control him, I know it."

Gideon's hand slips over mine, pulling at my fingers clutching my coffee cup. My attention turns toward him. "We will help him. I know you will find a way. All hope isn't lost just yet."

I smile at him, grateful for his reassurance. "I know. It's just hard not to worry with the way he looks."

At this point, Milo's skin is now an ashy grey. He's practically skin and bones, as if he doesn't eat. His eyes are dark and lifeless. And he moves like a reanimated corpse. All stiff and shuffling steps.

It's heart wrenching.

I squeeze my eyes shut and let the image fade from my mind.

Gideon stands from the table. "You need to allow yourself to rest before you try to save the world. Come on." His gentle words coax me from my seat. I join him at the head of the table. He pulls me into him, holding me tightly, filling me with his strength. I feel safe, powerful, stronger than ever.

My mind changes focus to the way his strong arms feel around me and how good it feels to be pressed against his muscled torso. He breathes in the scent of my hair and gently coaxes my face up to his.

His beautiful blue-green eyes search mine for something I can only guess at. There's a light in them that strikes me as hesitation. I suck in a breath, feeding into the strength bleeding into me, lifting up on my toes, and pressing my lips to his.

He breathes in deep as his lips move with mine. His arms tighten around me even more, and I softly moan with how good it feels to be this close to him.

I get lost in the moment. Lost in his kiss.

A sensation of weightlessness overcomes me, and I realize he is carrying me through his house. But I don't break from the kiss. It's too good. Too powerful. I don't care where we are going, as long as he is still kissing me.

A brief fall ends with my body pressed against a pillow-soft mattress and Gideon's weight resting on top of me. Even with all the movement, he continues to kiss me. His growing erection presses against my entrance and a rush of heat pools between my thighs, delighting in the way that he feels.

Gideon's fingers lace through my hair as he leans up taking a break from kissing me to catch his breath. I'm dizzy and lightheaded, and the way he looks hovering over me drives me absolutely *wild*.

A brief hesitation flashes through his eyes again, and I smile gently. "It's okay. We don't have to."

He shakes his head. "It's not that. I want to. Gods, I want to. I've waited so long for this moment. I just didn't think it would happen under these circumstances. So soon…"

It dawns on me that he's no longer headmaster.

There is absolutely *nothing* stopping us from just letting go and giving into each other now.

And that somehow makes everything so much more freeing.

"I want to savor this," he says, voice low and deep as he lowers himself to my lips again and leaves just one kiss there. A kiss on my chin. One on my jaw line, at the spot under my ear, the base of my neck.

Each time his lips touch my skin, warmth spreads and the ache for him continues to grow. Goosebumps prickle along my skin. I sigh. The sensation is simply *delicious*.

I too have waited for this moment, anticipating all the ways he would undo me and so much more.

His hands move to the seam of my shirt, inching his fingers under the hem to my skin burning at his slightest touch. Teasing the fabric farther up my torso.

Gently, slowly, he inches my shirt up, exposing my skin underneath. He pulls me up, slipping the shirt over my head. He casts it to the floor and takes a moment to enjoy everything that I offer him. It's delightful, the way he drinks me in, taking in every curve of my body.

"You're so amazingly beautiful," he murmurs as he runs his fingers from my chest, between my breasts, and to my belly button.

With him, I feel gorgeous. But I'll take amazingly beautiful any day.

I smile at him in response to his comment and grasp his shirt by the fistful, pulling him closer to me. He chuckles and obliges, kissing me and making me feel as though I am completely unstoppable.

With him, and my other men, I am.

I wrap my arms around his shoulders and soak in the comfort he gives me, while he sets my nerves on fire with every single touch. He takes his time as his fingers slide along my back, toward the strap of my bra. As he unsnaps the clips, I grip his shirt, tugging it over his head. I want to feel him pressed against me, unhindered by clothing, unhindered by rules, completely free. But I'm caught by the sight of his bare torso.

Curves of muscles angle over his shoulders, his pecs and his abs, his physique is like that of an athlete. And knowing what I know of Gideon, he's that and so much more.

I trace my fingers along the curves of his muscles, tracing the valleys that make up his form, and I love every single moment of it.

His skin is smooth, even with scars from the battles of his past, but they only add to the beauty of the man before me. A sense of pride fills me, and I'm so grateful he's mine. And I'm proud to also be his.

Now, there is no more need to hide. No more reason to hold back from what we both want. What we *need*. The time he takes, laying me down and sliding his hands down my sides, toward the waist of my jeans, leaving a trail of kisses as he moves, makes me feel coveted.

Soon, the button on my jeans is released, and he uses his teeth to unzip the zipper. I run my fingers through his hair, delighting in the feel. Carefully, he digs his fingers around the waistband of my pants and tugs them down my legs as he kneels between them.

Each move he makes is careful, calculated, purposeful.

As my jeans falls to the floor, he slaps them aside, sending them flying to the wall. Without missing a beat, he slides his hands along the outside of my legs and presses a kiss just above my sweet spot shielded by the cloth of my underwear, before climbing back up slowly.

I'm inching ever so sweetly toward release with just a touch. I bit the corner of my lower lip. Every move works to release the ache in my muscles. A little more of my stress fades away. I'm able to be fully present, relishing how he comforts me by worshiping every inch of my body. He deserves a little attention as well.

I wrap my left leg and arm around him, twisting and leaning my weight into him, until he's on his back. He smirks at me. "Look at you, using what you've been learning."

I shrug. "I've had some pretty good teachers."

He chuckles as I use my hands to trace the peaks and valleys of his muscles, inching down his legs to the waist band of his pants. I glance at him with a devious smile on my face and unsnap the button and slowly tug the zipper lower, allowing his erection to be unrestrained by the pants.

Once I've helped him out of his jeans, I slip off his boxer briefs, fully letting loose the massive erection he has. This man is *hung*.

I lick my lips in anticipation of being filled with him. Of him riding me into what I have always known would be an earth-shattering orgasm.

Hell, this man has already sent me through waves of intense pleasure with just a simple freaking touch. If his touch can do that to me, what's to come will unravel every thread of my reality and stitch them back together again.

I grip the shaft of his enormous cock and give it a few gentle strokes. Gideon groans, making me smile.

He unexpectedly snatches my wrist. "Not yet." His voice is gravely.

I meet his gaze and there's a hint of a plea in them. I nod, climbing over him, the tip of his erection sliding along my sensitive folds. I shudder in delight of the feel.

No sooner am I on top of him, getting ready to kiss him, does he flip me on my back. The sensation forces a chuckle from me. "That was fun."

"Hmm…" he muses. "Two can play this game."

"Touché." I smile.

He leans into me, the tip of his erection teasing my entrance and making me wiggle beneath him with hungry need. His mouth takes mine as his fingers find their way under the fabric of my underwear preventing him free rein. His slides them between the folds, brushing against my sensitive mound.

I gasp with pleasure.

He chuckles, continuing to stroke me to release. I cling to him as he sends me through wave after wave. As the end draws near, he tugs off my underwear like they are nothing, casting them to the side without a moment's thought.

He kisses me, long and deep, teasing my entrance

with the tip of his cock. His tip slides into my entrance, only to pull out. Entering me inch by inch, taking his time to stretch me until his entire length fills me. He settles between my legs as I widen them to give him full access to all of me.

It's beautiful, the way he makes love to me. He's gentle, taking his time, as he pushes inside me. He wants to savor this moment just as much as I do, and that makes my heart flutter in my chest.

We finally made it. We are finally able to give ourselves to the other completely.

The sensations that buzz through me leave tingles prickling over my skin. A moan escapes me, and I wrap my arms around him. He shudders a little at my touch and melts into me a little as he keeps up the pace.

It's euphoric, the things he's doing to me.

Soon, I reach another climax. He takes me through it so slowly, ensuring that not a single moment of our finally being together is rushed. We savor every moment of each other.

Three times more, I'm sent through waves of pleasure. This time, he stiffens, and I know he's letting himself release. He doesn't stop as hot liquid fills me, until my cries of pleasure no longer echo through the room.

OLIVIA ASH

He looks me in the eyes and there's so much love within them, it steals my breath away. "No one could ever keep me from you."

He kisses my forehead, the tip of my nose, and finally, my lips as he pulls out of me. He lays on his back with a heavy sigh. "That was amazing."

I chuckle. "You certainly exceeded my expectations." I tuck myself in next to him and he wraps an arm lovingly around me.

I'm so safe in his arms. So protected, loved, and strong.

Come what may, we've got this.

CHAPTER TWENTY-ONE

I stretch out my limbs, getting ready for Soren's class, watching him intently as he talks to Milo.

"What has been going on?" Soren asks him.

Milo shrugs. "Nothing."

"Come on, man. You've been skipping classes. That's not like you."

"Just didn't feel like coming," Milo says. He stands rigid, without his normal notebook. His hair is disheveled, and his glasses sit lower on the bridge of his nose. But he's not pushing them up like he normally does.

"You're even having Agatha pick up your work for you, but you don't turn it in." Soren shakes his head, arms crossed over his chest.

Jesse, standing to my right, leans in closer. "Sounds like Milo is due for an intervention."

I nod. "I think that's what's happening."

"Bout time," Savannah says from my left.

"Milo, this has gone on long enough. I want you to go to the infirmary and get checked out."

"No. I'm fine." Milo coldly stares at Soren. "I'm here by your orders."

My heart skips a few beats as I watch. I stop stretching because I don't know what's going to happen if Soren insists. Milo has been so out of character, that it wouldn't surprise me if he had to be dragged to the infirmary. And if that's the case, would Milo try to fight?

Soren may need help.

"Damn it, man. Go. That's all I'm asking." Soren gestures to the door. "Get a clean bill of health and then come back."

"After class," Milo says. His words are so unemotional and flat.

I frown at the interaction between two of my men. This could escalate soon. I should be ready to jump in and help.

"No. Go now and stay there. Or I will carry you myself." Soren drops his arms, ready to deliver on his promise of hauling Milo off.

"Fine." Milo slowly turns around and walks out the door.

I let out a breath I hadn't realized I was holding until that moment. There is something left of the Milo I know and love in there. Or, at the very least, he still has enough sense to know that Soren never makes idle threats. He made the right decision to avoid that.

I'm relieved, but only to an extent. This is far from over. There is only so much the infirmary can do. It will buy us some time, for sure. Hopefully enough to find whatever it is we need to reverse this.

Soren sighs and heads to the center of the classroom. I resume my stretching.

Dummies stand in five groups of about ten, taking up the wall behind Soren. Today, we're probably going to do exercises with them. But Soren has yet to discuss them.

"We're doing the signal, right?" Savannah quietly asks. I had caught up with her in the hallway just before class to let her know I had information about Milo that needed to be shared with our group.

I nod.

"Let's hope he remembers," Jesse adds. He leans against the wall, casually waiting for the instructions to start as the rest of the class is stretching themselves.

"If everyone is limber, we'll begin," Soren says,

stepping to the center of the class. "Ms. Blackwood, come here, please."

I nod and jog toward him. Once I'm at his side, he faces the rest of the class. "We're going to practice defending ourselves against multiple opponents using both hand-to-hand combat and magic." He gestures to me. "Miss Blackwood will demonstrate."

Oh good. I get to be the guinea pig.

"White, defensive magic only," he says to me. "Don't want anything catching on fire."

I nod.

Soren steps back, joining the wall of students and with a snap of his fingers, brings ten of the dummies to life. These ones are covered in basic armor, wooden shields, swords, and helmets. Their straw-filled underbellies are only protected by a thin strip of wood with painted targets. Their faces are painted with rudimentary circles and lines for eyes and mouths. They move toward me, surrounding me in a circle.

I take a deep breath and take a fighting stance, preparing for what I've trained to do so many times before.

The first one attacks at my right. I block the advance by holding out my palm toward it and blasting it with white light. A second one advances from my left while a third approaches from behind. I side kick the one to my left and roundhouse the sword from the third's wooden hands. It flies off toward the other end of the classroom. Now that this dummy is disarmed, I blast it with white magic as well, then face the final seven. Four advance me at the same time. They head straight for me.

I quickly duck the attack of the first, narrowly missing the swing of the sword aimed for my neck. Keeping up the momentum, as I crouch, I stick out my leg, knocking back a second dummy. I blast the third with white light, and as I stand back up on my feet, block the blow from the sword with my left arm, delivering a powerful punch to its torso. I wrap my arm around the one with the sword, pulling it closer to me, as it stabs into the fourth approaching from behind me.

With a back kick, that one is knocked to the ground, and while the final three begin their advance, I blast the dummy's head off with my magic. Facing the final three as they come closer, I conjure my shield and aim my handful of magic toward them.

Not backing down, they come at me at full force.

I wasn't expecting that.

The first of the three is thrown back by my magic as the other two break away from their formation to come at me from both sides.

I'm used to training with dummies that are slow and tactful. These, however, mean business.

One gets a cheap shot with a sword smack to my back while the other smacks me in the leg.

I glare at Soren who is watching with a stern expression. He nods once, very slowly. Anger fills me. If he wants a demonstration, I'll give him one.

Fire courses along my skin. A series of hushed murmurs fills the room. I face the two dummies readying for their attack. One has its sword held above its head, preparing to bring it down on my skull. While the other is braced for a nice jab to my torso.

I drop my shield.

Magic fills my hands and I aim them both off to the side of me. Once my magic is ready to spill over, I release it, blasting the two dummies into cinders and dust.

As soon as the debris settles, I face Soren who looks irritated that I destroyed his precious dummies. I shrug.

"Join the rest of your class," he snaps.

"Fine." I take my place between Jesse and Savannah.

Savannah smiles at me and nudges me with her elbow, "Nice work."

"That's my girl," Jesse says. "I knew you would find a way to show up Soren eventually."

Chuckles erupt from Jesse's comment.

Soren huffs angrily as he stands at the center of the class. "If you want, you may take on twenty of them."

"And make you look bad?" Jesse answers. "I wouldn't dream of it."

"If you're quite done, can you explain why defeating multiple opponents would be important?" He glares at Jesse who is not affected in the very least. Guess he's still in a bad mood after reprimanding Milo.

One student raises his hand. He's quite a timid guy, I think he belongs in House of Winterwolf.

"Yes," Soren says, calling on him.

He stammers, but eventually gets it out. "To survive, because not every fight is going to be one on one?"

Soren nods. "Close."

I raise my hand, but Soren overlooks me to call on another student. "You?"

"It's important," a female's voice says, "to know how to gauge weaknesses and use them to your advantage. How to predict movements and surroundings."

"Closer still." Soren looks over the line of students, completely ignoring my hand again. "Fighting multiple opponents is bound to happen at some point or another, whether at war, or defending a defenseless victim. It's important to understand not only how to fight multiple enemies, but when to recognize impending defeat and look for an escape."

"What about the harpy eagles? What if one of them turns mad with the plague?" A student I can't see asks.

Soren's frown perfectly captures my own feelings over Headmaster Westbrook's arrangement with Agatha's father. All these students know is that the plague is spreading, and news of what happened on Crimson Isles may not have stayed contained. And with the sudden temporary shelter provided for Demitri Collins's harpy eagles on our island, there's no wonder they're beginning to ask questions.

Soren clears his throat. "This is another good reason. Because unusual opponents like the harpy eagles tend to fight in groups. Never one on one. Defending yourself is a means of survival."

"Boring," Jesse says, yawning.

Soren's eyes damn near alight with fire. "Mr. Taylor, that's enough."

"We'll see," Jesse says, voice low. I chuckle, trying to hide it behind my hand, but it's no use.

Savannah raises her hand. "Is that the point of this class? To teach us what we should already know? Do you not have anything real to show us?"

Soren's eyes widen as if he didn't expect Savannah to ever make such a comment. Steam is practically spewing from his nose as he huffs.

I chuckle harder.

"I think we're giving him a complex," Jesse says.

A light flashes through Soren's gaze. One of realization. I think he finally caught on to what we're doing.

"I want you three to stand off to the side. The rest of the class may begin practicing. Watch your opponent's movements and predict what their next move will be."

The last of the groups of ten dummies are broken up into threes, and the students line up before each group.

Savannah, Jesse, and I move off to the side, to a corner where no one can overhear us.

"There are other means of getting my attention than showing off in class," Soren hisses.

I shrug. "We had to be as discreet as possible without giving it away. Did you really forget about the signal?"

Soren pinches the bridge of his nose. "Laps. All three of you. Once class is done, we'll leave."

We all three nod and start jogging around the room.

When class is over, I'm sweaty and exhausted from the constant laps. I think that was the point though. Show the other students Soren won't tolerate insubordination and using us as an example of what will happen if the class isn't taken seriously.

As the last student leaves, Soren approaches us. "Let's go."

We follow him to the secret place our meetings have been held. Lady Alene is already there, and waiting for us, which I'm grateful for. She must have seen us approaching. Once Jesse sets the illusion, I pull out the book and share the information I found out with Gideon's help.

"This is the curse Milo was put under. It's called the *Corpus Et Animam*." I turn the page and point to the next one behind it, where the bottom half is ripped off. "And of course, the cure is probably crumpled up and in a trash heap by now."

"I recognize that name." Savannah shakes her head as if she's trying to shake lose the exact memory. "I overheard my father mention it once when I was younger." Her eyebrows pull together as though she's having difficulty recalling exactly. Eventually, she sighs. "I'll message him as soon as possible. He may know what we need to break the curse."

"I know," I say. "It's a degenerative mind control

curse. It requires an item to be enchanted with the blood of whom it's meant to control."

"Not to mention," Soren says with a frustrated sigh, "nearly unbreakable, from what we've seen."

"But not impossible," I add. "Agatha's necklace, that is what was used for the curse."

"Yeah," Jesse adds, "But getting it off of her is going to be a challenge."

Soren nods. "We can do it if we are very careful."

"What I want to know is how she was able to get Milo's blood in the first place. Not only that, but how Agatha was able to turn Milo against me."

Savannah shakes her head. "I'm not sure. It's a very dark spell, and it's so powerful. There's absolutely no way for her to have done it on her own."

"You're right," I add. "Caseus helped her."

Soren's eyebrows knit together. "That guy never struck me as someone who has any dark intentions."

"That could be the point," I say. "No one looks twice at an unassuming cook. How much do you want to bet he's working with the Order as well?"

And Agatha is playing along, thinking she's getting everything she wants without consequence.

"Agatha is naïve and short-sighted if she thinks this curse is going to grant her Milo with no repercussions," Savannah says. "Regardless, he's running out of time. I'll message my father immediately. The window of opportunity to save him is closing. I…" She hesitates to finish, snapping her mouth shut and dropping her gaze to the ground.

"What is it?" I ask.

She shakes her head. "He'll be dead within the month."

"Then we better get started," I say, determined not to let that outcome happen. I'll be damned.

"How do you propose we do this?" Jesse asks. "Want me to go upturning every wastebasket in the castle?"

I shake my head. "I have to speak with Professor Croswell again. Now that we know it's the *Corpus Et Animam*, I'm sure she's studied it and can help."

"That's worked well before in the past," Jesse mutters.

"She's been busy trying to find a cure for the plague. I've tried to stop by a couple of times before, but she's either been out, or refused visitors. I think at this point, she'll be more inclined to help us. She *has* to."

"It will be too conspicuous to immediately head there after meeting with me, especially since I've just sent Milo to the infirmary. If Caseus is spying on is, we don't know who else could be as well."

"Then I'll go after my last class."

Lady Alene's bright eyes observe us. Sometimes I wonder what's on her mind. "Your plan sounds solid," she says. "However, I must urge you to be extremely cautious. Our new headmaster does not sit well with me. He appears charismatic and kind, and usually a new headmaster calls on me often for advice and information. However, he has only spoken to me once, and that was to tell me that his office and private room are off-limits."

Why am I not surprised?

"That makes two of us," I say. "We'll be as careful as possible. Thank you, Lady."

She nods graciously.

For a moment, I'm tempted to breach the topic of the vision I had when I last touched her hand. I wonder if the ivy leaf charm she gave me to help me sleep also imparted some type of magical impression from her. But time is of the essence, and we have to work under the assumption we're being watched like we were during Gideon's investigation. I make a mental note to speak candidly with her on this once we take care of Milo and get Gideon reinstated.

"I think it's safe to say that the headmaster doesn't sit well with our entire group," Soren adds.

"A fact that you have kept less than hidden," I add.

He shrugs.

"Once I hear back from my dad," Savannah says, "I can also make sure we're going about curing Milo correctly and not making any mistakes."

"Good, but we'll still need an expert present to help with the prep," Soren says. "You take the book and gather the supplies needed. We'll need Crosswell on board for this. Jesse, find a place in secret that can take the prepping without being found."

"His lab would work. Or his room," I offer.

Jesse smirks. "I noticed he hasn't been using the lab. The room may be tricky, especially with how close Agatha is."

Good point.

I nod. "Then the lab it is. Make sure you add some extra protections and wards."

He smiles. "Gladly."

I have a feeling that if anyone were to stumble upon Milo's lab, it would be a painful experience. Just judging by the dark glint in Jesse's eyes and the way there is hidden meaning in the word he just spoke.

"Wren, see what you can do to get that necklace from Agatha. But be careful. I can't save you if you get caught."

"Then it's a damn good thing I'm not planning on getting caught."

CHAPTER TWENTY-TWO

As planned, once my final class is dismissed, I head for Professor Crosswell's office. I catch her right as she is leaving for the day. She faces me with a startled expression.

"Ms. Blackwood. What can I do for you?"

"I need to speak with you in private. It's urgent."

She looks around and checks her watch. "Is this life or death?"

I nod.

"Your friend?"

"Milo's not just a friend, but yes."

She sighs and leans into the door frame as though she's completely exhausted. After a few moments she opens her eyes. "Very well."

She unlocks the door to her office and invites me

in. I follow her to her desk and take a seat in one of the high back office chairs situated in front of her desk. Her lab table is cluttered with test tubes and other devices, which makes me wonder if she's any closer to a cure than she was before.

"What is it you need?" Professor Crosswell's voice pulls my attention back to her. I pull out the book and set it on the desk in front of her. "What's this?"

"The marked page is the curse that was placed on Milo."

The corners of her lips pull downward as she glances at the page listing the *Corpus Et Animam*. "Are you certain?"

I nod, lips pressed into a firm line.

She leans back in her seat and curses under her breath. "Whoever let that curse fall into the hands of a student will have hell to pay."

"Tell me about it," I say, turning the page so she can see that the section with the cure has been ripped out. "But right now, Milo is the one suffering. He needs our help."

She shakes her head. "I'm sorry, Ms. Blackwood. With as much time that has lapsed, in order to reverse a curse like this, it would take something I would never encourage a student to do."

My heart sinks a little. "Why? What do I have to do?"

She studies me for a few moments. "First, I want to apologize. I wish I would've caught this sooner. I was so wrapped up in my own problems with the plague that I forgot my duty here to you... and to Milo. If this really is the curse that was placed on him, then I know what will break it. However, it will take something irrevocable. Virtually, it would bind the two of you together for life."

I don't see a downside to this. "Okay, and?"

She sighs, closing the book and sliding it back to me. "Decisions like this should be made extremely carefully, with the pros and cons considered."

"Why not just come out and tell me what it is?" I ask, growing more frustrated. I don't have the time for this. And neither does Milo.

"It's requires a blood oath." Her words resonate with the weight of her warning. "It took blood to make the curse, and it will take blood to break it. Only the breaking is a permanent decision."

"I understand. I'll do it."

Professor Crosswell raises an eyebrow and leans forward, apparently less than convinced. "You are young. You may be in love with him now, but nothing in the rules says you will be years later down the road.

You are virtually binding yourself to Milo for the rest of your life. If something happens, you will continue to be bound to him. It's like marriage, without the convenience of divorce. You are essentially tattooing your name on his body, without permission."

I listen as she explains. Her voice is calm, smooth, and patient. I get the enormity of the decision I need to make, but in my mind, it's already made. I'll do this blood oath. Damn the consequences.

"I just want you to understand fully what you'll be getting yourself into. Know that there is no undoing this once it's done."

"You don't know a thing about me or my men. Or the lengths I would go to in order to save them."

"I too have more than one lover, and I would go to the ends of the earth for them." She regards me with a look of understanding. "Very well, then. I'll help. Where did you even find this book?"

"In the restricted section of the library."

"The restricted section? And how did you get in there?"

I quickly switch the focus off me. "Caseus the cook has a counterfeit key, by the way. He gave Agatha Collins that curse, and she probably thought it was a simple mind control spell to get Milo to fall in love with her."

Her eyes widen, and I can tell that she's pieced something together with that little bit of information. "That explains so much."

I cock my head to the side, eyebrows drawing together. "How so?"

She sets her gaze on me. "Well, for one, it's impossible for the key to be counterfeit. It wouldn't work. The safeguards are much more clever than that. However, I did believe I misplaced my key for a short time. I needed it to return the books I borrowed on possible cures for the plague." She waves a dismissive hand in front of her. "Anyway, I found it in my desk drawer. I believed I was so frazzled and sleep-deprived, that I had forgotten where I had placed it."

"I see."

"Thank you. Now, I know it was Caseus who took it. He has no business or authority to go in there."

"I thought the same thing," I say.

She levels her gaze on me that silently says, I had no business being in there either. I smile and shrug.

"I'll report the cook to the headmaster."

I snort. She looks at me with a confused expression.

"He's no better."

"What do you mean? How do you know?" She folds her hands over the top of her desk, leaning forward, keeping her voice low, as though there is someone close by, listening in on our conversation.

"There are Order spies here in the school. I believe Headmaster Westbrook is one of them. You could tell him about Caseus, just don't be surprised when nothing happens."

"Hmm..." she leans back in her seat, dropping her hands to her lap. "Now that you mention it, there is something... off about him that I couldn't quite place. And yesterday when I tried to get his input on my plague research, he actually told me I was fighting a lost cause. And the look in his eye, wasn't one of hopelessness, but—"

"Let me guess," I say, "one of smug triumph?"

She frowns. "Yes. I think in that moment his mask slipped a little. Very well, I won't talk to Westbrook about the cook. How is Milo doing?"

I huff a heavy breath. "Still in the infirmary. We're doing everything we can to slow it down enough to buy us time."

She nods and takes out a piece of paper and quickly scribbles down a list of items. Once finished, she replaces the pen and slides the paper over to me. "I'll go check on him immediately."

I glance at the paper and instantly recognize the items. "Is this...?"

She nods. "Good luck, Ms. Blackwood. You'll need it."

"Thank you so much," I say jumping up from the chair. I pick up the book and head for the library. Without time to spare, I have to be on top of this as much as possible.

I feel better knowing Professor Crosswell is finally on board with me and my team. Even though I'm a bit nervous about the blood oath, I will sacrifice anything and everything for the men I love.

With the list of the things we need. Now, it's possible to save Milo.

I understand what it means to bind myself to Milo for the rest of my life. Though that may seem like a terrible fate to some, I know my men. This isn't just some short-lived fancy. In many ways, we are already bound for life.

Because of my meteorite, they were chosen for me. My magic reacts to them and theirs to me.

We are bonded.

I can't lose Milo. The thought of that becoming a reality hurts like hell. Like my heart is being ripped from my chest. It's like my soul is being pulled from me.

Whatever is needed to save him, consider it done.

He deserves so much more than withering away like he is.

I reach the library in what feels like record time. I stop at the door and take a few breaths to collect myself before stepping inside. I know what I need to do, and it's about time I get started.

Savannah and Jesse are in the library, sitting at the same table, but at opposite ends. I catch them whispering to each other, and it's clear that they are trying to keep up the guise of working separately.

I join Jesse, sitting across from him. I smile at him, but address Savannah. "What did your dad say?"

"Have you heard of a blood oath?" she asks.

Jesse smirks, but it lacks all humor.

"Just now, yes. Crosswell is helping." I twist in my seat a little. "It's good to know we're on the right track."

"Is that what Professor Crosswell is having you work on?" Savannah asks.

I nod slightly. Enough for her to catch it. "She gave me a list of items to gather for the ritual. Can you help? I figure being a healer and all, and with your dad's support, you can get these more quickly than me."

Besides, there's a necklace I need to snatch off someone's scrawny neck.

"I can do it," Savannah whispers.

Meanwhile, Jesse and I hold hands, talking, putting on a show as though we hadn't noticed Savannah was there to begin with.

"You really think this is a good idea?" Jesse asks. "Savannah's father told her that a blood oath is—"

"Unbreakable," I finish. "I know."

He smirks. "Quite devoted, aren't you?"

I shrug. "I would do it for all of you."

He laughs under his breath. "We would do the same for you. In a heartbeat."

I smile. "I know."

"Pssst…" Savannah says toward Jesse. "Want to help me grab the items on the list? We can split it half-and-half, so no one will wonder why I'm getting all these things alone."

"I love a good challenge," Jesse says.

"Good." There's a moment of silence, and I can almost sense the hesitation in Savannah.

"What is it?" I ask.

"The oath is a binding ritual. It doesn't just make you bound to him, it practically joins your soul with his. This is a ritual that is only done in the direst of cases and usually never works out well for the person giving it."

"Why?" I ask.

"Because, the person having the spell placed on them doesn't normally have the ability to give permission for it."

"I'm not worried," I say. Milo will understand. I'm sure of it.

Jesse rests his hand on the small of my back. "Whatever it takes."

"Agreed." I sigh with relief. We're getting closer.

I realize there is a light at the end of the tunnel. I know this blood oath is the right thing to do.

Jesse nods to me, rubs the back of my hand with reassurance, and pulls Professor Crosswell's list toward him, which has been face-down on the table. Jesse slyly picks it up and heads out of the room. Soon, Savannah stands up, whispers, "Good luck," and leaves as well.

Hold on Milo. We're not giving up.

CHAPTER TWENTY-THREE

I'm halfway to Soren's office, weaving through the halls as quickly as I can. Now that Jesse and Savannah are gathering the items we need for the ritual, we can start setting things in motion. I'm so much closer to helping Milo, and every second counts.

Hang in there, I'm not giving up on you.

I pick up my pace.

A loud roar and crashing boom hits the castle, vibrating the walls. Dust and debris fly across the hall just ahead of me, and I brace myself against a wall. My startled gaze sweeps the area around me, searching for the source of the commotion.

A few first-years behind me cry out in shock. Another deafening boom resonates throughout the castle. A girl that I recognize from Professor Crosswell's class rushes past me, brown eyes wide with fear. My heart pounds in my chest when I notice cracks in the wall, spidering toward the ceiling where small chunks fall off, hitting the floor.

I yank a first-year student hard into my chest right before a bigger piece of ceiling lands on his head. That was close.

It doesn't take long before screaming echoes through the halls as students rush through the chaos of what is now overcoming my home.

Magical megaphones instantly appear in the halls, all of them announcing the same thing. "All students report to the stronghold beneath the castle immediately. Proceed in a calm and orderly fashion."

Flashing, iridescent lights hover in the hall like arrows, pointing students in the right direction. I'm almost tempted to follow, but not even this will keep me from reaching Milo and helping him.

I rush across the hall toward the window to see if I can figure out what is going on. Another crash, and the castle walls crumble a little more. After bracing myself through the impact, I'm able to look out and witness a mob of harpy eagles attacking the school.

It's like nothing I've ever seen.

Some of these creatures swoop in and land in the courtyard and on top of towers, dealing damage with their sharp talons and storm-wielding powers. Others circle the gardens in order to stalk and carry away anyone still outside. I gasp in shock when two lightning-quick eagles crash into each other mid-air, each slashing at the other with their beaks.

Just like the eaglet that had attacked me and Soren, the eagles' eyes are focused on their prey, their crowns of feathers spread out in an intimidating fashion, and by the look of the sky, they're brewing up one hell of a storm.

Damn Agatha and her father. All they've brought to this island is trouble.

The announcement blares again over the crowd of frantic students. One of them slams into me, nearly knocking me off of my feet. I manage to catch myself on the windowsill, and no sooner than I turn to check on the student that crashed into me, they're gone.

I notice a few professors trying to corral the masses toward the stronghold beneath the castle.

I look out the window again and notice that, at the edge of the island, a few harpy eagles are huddled together. They aren't attacking. They aren't stalking students, or launching lightning and wind, but are instead lounging in their designated field, as if nothing were amiss. Clearly the giant birds attacking the school and each other aren't like the ones at the edge of the island.

I think I know the reason why, but trying to see if my suspicion is correct couldn't have come at a worse time. Milo needs me, and in the middle of this dangerous attack, he needs me more than ever.

I pull away from the window and head toward the courtyard. Knowing Soren and his skills, as well as his strong sense of protection, he's more than likely trying to cover any students still stuck outside. I dip low and cover my nose with the crook of my elbow as another crash rockets through the castle, sending more stone and debris crashing all around me. I make it to the exit and through the open doorway and see Soren battling it out with harpy eagles, joined by some of the other professors and students in their last year.

"Take them to the stronghold! I'll hold off the harpies!" He quickly motions to the four professors with him. They eye him with hesitance and doubt, but they finally comply and gather the students with them, leading them away from the fight.

I love his bravery. But damn it, he's going to get himself killed.

I can't let Soren fight these eagles without my help. It would kill me if something were to happen to him. Besides, there's not going to be a way to help Milo if the castle falls down around him. The harpy eagles have to be taken care of first.

Passing over the threshold and making it into the courtyard, I put up a shield and carefully approach Soren. With swiftness and grace, he rolls and dodges a harpy eagle zooming in toward him with its gleaming talons. He rises to his feet and blasts it with fire, then quickly constructs burning ropes of fire with his magic, using them like whips to smack two other harpies and force them back.

The harpy eagles, in their rage, bring down the storm they've been brewing. Booming thunder resounds above the courtyard, lightning careens against the castle, and torrential rain and hail crash down. Soren throws up a shield over himself just in time to avoid being smashed by icy rocks. A huge chunk of stone crashes down into the courtyard from above. The castle is slowly being destroyed, and all I can do is hope that all of the students are now safe in the stronghold. I silently pray Milo is secure in the infirmary and Crosswell is keeping watch over him until we get there.

Assuming he's still there. At this point, they may have even decided to move infirmary patients to the stronghold.

I shake my head and focus on helping Soren. I rush forward and join him, feeding more energy and strength into my shield.

As I reach him, he becomes encased in flames. I pause and watch in awe as the fire encompassing him grows in strength. This is going to exhaust him. I've never seen him perform such a powerful spell like this before.

The heat billows toward me, and the ground he stands on becomes charred within a five-foot radius. I take a few steps back to avoid getting burned. A few more seconds of him building up his power, eyes focused on the birds surrounding us, and he releases pillars of flames that shoot out in all directions.

It hits some of the birds, while others squawk and fly away toward another spot on the island. At least, for now, they are away from the courtyard.

He faces me as he works to catch his breath, both of us dropping our shields now that we are no longer in danger of being pelted by rain, hail, or zapped by lightning.

"We're ready to do the ritual for Milo. Jesse and

Savannah are going to meet us there." I quickly push out the words.

He nods as a girl's scream reaches us from somewhere beneath the debris of the castle.

"Go. I'll meet you there." He scans the area of debris, looking for a sign of the poor girl trapped under the rubble. "I need to help her."

I hesitate, not really wanting to leave him. His spell to push back the harpy eagles worked, which takes him out of immediate danger. Finally, I nod and head back inside.

Anxious to make it to Milo, I turn down the hallway, and I crash into Headmaster Westbrook. He grabs me by the shoulders to steady me, and I instinctively pull away to create some space between us.

His expensive grey suit is soiled and torn, probably after an encounter with a harpy or the storm, but despite that, he looks pleased. A little too pleased. With the way a satisfactory glint flashes through his eyes upon seeing me, I realize something is wrong.

"Miss Blackwood, I was just looking for you," he says, smiling charmingly like it's an enchantment that brings most women to their knees. Well, it may work on most women, but I'm certainly *not* most women.

"Headmaster Westbrook, I swear I'm on my way to

the stronghold. I was just helping Professor McCallister."

He doesn't have to know where I'm really going. I start to make my way past him, and he grabs my arm, pulling me back to stand in front of him.

"Not so fast," he says, releasing my arm. "The stronghold is that way." He points in the opposite direction I'm headed in.

Great. Just freaking great.

"I can help. I can make sure there are no stragglers," I say, standing my ground.

He eyes me up and down. "Oh, I think I've found the straggler. Trying to be a hero, are we? Come with me, Ms. Blackwood."

I shudder as an odd warmth with a slight electrical bite travels up my legs and reaches my belly. Against my will, my legs turn me around and start marching in the direction the headmaster had indicated. I grunt and try to regain control of my legs, trying to will them to stop and obey me, but it's no use.

God damn this asshole.

"Shouldn't you be out there taking care of those harpy eagles that *you* allowed onto our island?" He falls into step with me, walking side-by-side as if I were a willing participant in our strides. I eye some of the adjoining halls we pass, wondering if I can regain control of my legs and then run down one of them.

"I wouldn't do that, if I were you," Headmaster Westbrook says, looking over at me. "It won't bode well."

"This is all your fault. I wouldn't be surprised if you wanted this to happen." I try to redirect my feet, and a sharp pain shoots up my calves.

He smirks. "The birds are being taken care of well enough. Most if not all the other students are in the stronghold. I have a separate task for you."

What could this man possibly want from me? "You could have said that instead of threatening me."

He chuckles. "As headmaster, I shouldn't have to ask more than once. I'm a patient man, Ms. Blackwood. But challenge my authority, and I become much less patient."

If you say so.

As we head toward Gideon's—well, now this guy's —office, I'm torn. My heart plummets a little in my chest, because I'm still carrying some guilt over Gideon being removed from his spot as headmaster. But the one comfort I take solace in is the night he and I shared. That blissful, amazing, mind-blowing night where I was wrapped in his arms, riding him through wave after wave of pure ecstasy. And if I want to see him again, as well as Milo and the others, I need to break this hold Westbrook has over me and get back to business.

Confusion sets in as we walk past the hall leading to the headmaster's office. My legs stiffen with pain as I march along with him.

I side-eye him.

He glances at me again, a gleam of greed in his eyes. A look I've seen a thousand times in the eyes of trolls when they've captured a prize.

I begin reaching deep down to my core, coaxing a subtle burning energy from my meteorite.

I don't know if you can understand me, I tell the meteorite that had fused with me when I was five years old, *but no one forces me to go where I don't want. And I'm guessing you feel the same. I need my legs back.*

"Where are we going?" I ask over the blaring magical megaphones that are still giving out their announcement.

I suck in a deep breath as the stiff force of Westbrook's spell slightly fades.

"You'll see." His words softly carry over the disarray.

Oh, goody. I just *love* surprises.

Not.

My feet feel as if they're on fire, but I'm able to wiggle my toes.

Hell yes.

The headmaster halts and places his hands on the wall. Magic burst from beneath them, brilliant dark blue with specks of silver and a cloudlike mist of black. I arch an eyebrow. He turns to face me. "Come with me."

I stare into the pit of the hidden passage, and my instant response is, "No, thank you."

Headmaster Westbrook leans toward me, closing the gap enough that I can feel his breath on my face. "I'm not playing around, girl."

I catch two figures rounding the corner in my peripheral.

"Hey, over here!" I yell out, hoping the attention of witnesses would force Westbrook to back off.

Unfortunately, it turns out to be Agatha and the cook, Caseus Demont. They head straight toward me and the headmaster. Agatha smiles at me, looking for all the world like nothing is currently being destroyed as we stand in the halls, in danger of being crushed by rubble falling from the ceiling. And Caseus? He looks at me triumphantly.

The headmaster's expression contorts into one of

fury as he follows my gaze to them. "What the hell are you two doing here? I gave you explicit orders."

Oh, interesting. It seems I'm not the only one being insubordinate.

I flex my left foot. I can feel my legs again. Thank the gods.

"Just making sure the girl doesn't give you any troubles," the cook responds.

Oh, fabulous. They're talking about me. And I have a feeling I know why.

"I've got it covered, now stick to the plan," Headmaster Westbrook says. He faces me, smiling in a less charming and more threatening way. "Play nice and come along, like a good girl."

Girl? That's twice he's called me that.

The audacity.

"Never." I know enough by now to know exactly where this is heading. And I'm not liking this one bit. "Not until you tell me what the hell is going on here."

"Finishing what we started," the cook says, wearing an expression as if he's just won the lottery.

I level my gaze on the cook. "Finishing what?"

"Fool!" Headmaster Westbrook snaps at the cook.

"Finish what, exactly?" I ask.

The headmaster backhands me across my face. The

sting of his slap makes me bite my tongue. I'm seeing stars.

This bastard.

The cook shrugs, an arrogant grin on his face. "It's not like she isn't going to find out."

"I can take care of her," Agatha says, stepping forward with her chin lifted into the air. "Get us out of here before the castle crumbles around us."

I glare at her. "I already kicked your ass. Are you sure you want a second round?"

She balls her fists, her annoying little face scrunched up in anger. But she doesn't make a move against me. Probably because Westbrook has a look of murder on his face as he shoves a finger in the direction of the opposite wall, a silent order for her to stand aside.

She backs off, settling herself against the wall, watching with a sickening degree of gratification as the headmaster grabs me by the arm and pulls me toward the secret opening I have no desire to go through. I wonder if even Gideon knew this hidden passageway exists. If I survive through this, I'll have to ask.

A piece of rock nearly lands on her pretty little head. She squeals as she jumps out of the way. I smirk.

Serves her right.

A piece of falling debris nearly misses the headmaster's arm by an inch.

Damn. So close.

"Time to go," he says, shoving me toward the dark opening.

I plant my legs firmly and deliver a hard jab to his face. Let him see how he likes getting hit.

The headmaster stumbles, and I break away from his grasp. I take a few steps back in order to put space between us—and the dark passageway.

"Girl, we only want back what you have stolen. Come. All I want is the meteorite."

He just told me all I needed to know.

Everything they've done, taking my men away from me, causing this chaos at the castle, was for this moment. To get me alone. To take me, and ultimately the source of my unique power.

"What part of finders keepers are you having a hard time with?" I ask, crouching into my fighting stance.

He knows there's no way to separate me from the meteorite without harming or killing me. There's no way I'm going with him. At least we now have confirmation the Order is here. Gideon had said he couldn't read some of those that were here. Now we know why.

I blast the headmaster with my magic, a bolt of white light shooting from my right palm, aimed for his left shoulder. He dodges it with a swift tilt, and he stares at me, a dangerous glint in his eyes. Agatha and Caseus close in, joining him as backup. Magic crackles along their hands and arms, and Agatha especially looks eager to use hers.

This is either going to be a really clever escape, or end up really, really bad.

CHAPTER TWENTY-FOUR

A thunderous boom claps against the castle. A harpy eagle crashes halfway through a nearby window and shrieks. By its movements and the thrusts of its beak, I can tell it's fighting another harpy eagle. The giant bird squawks and then flies away, apparently giving chase to its opponent. Part of the ceiling near the window caves in, sending large pieces of stone crashing to the floor.

My heart sinks at the destruction of my home as it's being reduced to rubble. At the idea that these three people in front of me are keeping me from Milo. But I will be useless if they capture me. I'll die if they take my power away.

And that sure as hell isn't going to happen.

Maybe I should carry a sign as a warning to other Order members. One that says, "No touchy."

I know from recent experience, facing off with the Order is no simple task. And I'm not nearly powerful enough to stop two of them in addition to Agatha, who simply wants to kill me. At least, not with my conduit on. It's a risk I'm willing to take, but if I don't beat them and get out of here, I'm screwed, and Milo's as good as dead.

Discreetly, I tuck my hands behind me and slip off my wristband, tucking it into the back of my waist band.

If it's a fight they want, it's a fight they are going to get, and they aren't going to believe what hit them.

Headmaster Westbrook huffs out a heavy breath as his hands fill with deep blue magic mixed with black smoky veins. "I've had enough of this!"

I smirk. "Bring it."

He launches a powerful ball of light toward me. As it hurls toward me, I quickly crouch low. The blast of magic soars just above my head, singeing my copper red hair.

Caseus hurls balls of even darker magic, almost black with a deep purple tint, toward my head. I dodge the attack as both of the balls of his magic merges together, creating one large ball of destruction. It hits the side of the castle, blasting a large hole into the wall. I watch the rubble fall away with a frown. It was a close call. A hair slower, and I would be done for.

No longer constricted by my conduit, I feed my energy, my anger, and desperation into a brilliant ball of fire and lightning. The force of it is so strong that I actually feel my feet lift up and I'm hovering inches above the ground. The crackling blue lightning extends from my ball and weaves itself around me, almost like a shield.

Both Caseus and Headmaster Westbrook's eyes widen in shock. The cook looks hesitant, and he throws up a shield to protect himself. The headmaster creates a dark mist in front of him for added protection, though I can still see his face through the screen of smoke. He's not afraid like Caseus. He's actually gleeful. He actually believes he's going to win this fight and take my power.

I hurl my ball of fire and lightning toward them, and it crashes against their shields, breaking them instantly and burning their flesh. They both scream out in pain and fall to the ground. My gaze rakes my surroundings. Two down, one to go. I spot Agatha hiding around the corner of a hall, poking her head out and watching with wide eyes.

Coward.

Caseus is still writhing on the ground, his arms darkened and bloody. Headmaster Westbrook is steadying himself as he's getting back on his feet.

My time to escape is either now or never.

As blasts of dark magic sail toward me from the headmaster, I make a bee line for the hole in the wall leading outside. It'll be a rough landing, but at least I'll be okay enough to face those three again. This is not over. As I jump feet first through the hole, I hear the headmaster angrily shout.

Serves him right.

I'm not the *girl* he thinks I am.

I sail through the air, dropping about twenty feet. As I land, I crouch and roll to ease the impact of the fall. I jump to my feet and see Soren still in the court-yard. Anger rises within me at seeing him still out here. He was supposed to be inside with the others.

Instead, he's off about one-hundred feet to the left, still blasting his fire at harpy eagles. Jesse and Savannah are standing with him now, working side-by-side, taking them down with spells that run through them like sharp swords. One harpy eagle is nearly decapitated by Jesse and Savannah's coordinated spells, and another's wings are mangled by a combined blast from them.

All around them the giant bird bodies fall, riddling

the ground with puddles of blood and bone. It's a gruesome sight, but as much damage as they're dealing, more eagles show up to the fight.

I rush to make it toward them, finding a few of the harpy eagle bodies joining the ranks of the fallen not far from where we stand.

"Don't tell me you all came back here for me." I create another fire-lightning ball, like I did earlier with the headmaster, and let it loose on two harpy eagles gliding above us.

"You can't get rid of us that easily," Jesse says with a wink.

Of course.

My irritation fades and is slowly replaced with a grin. I love these guys.

"These ones are infected with the plague," Savannah says as she shoots another bird, clipping its wing. It spins and crashes into one of the towers, screeching in agony as it tries in futility to regain its flight.

"We need to take them out as fast as we can," Soren says.

"We'll finish off the remaining ones," I say, shouting over the intense storm winds.

From this side, I get a better picture. The total number of harpy eagles was twenty-five. If three of them remain unaffected on the other side of the island, sticking to themselves, and about fourteen of them lie in still heaps on the ground, that leaves about eight that are still in the sky.

Not great odds.

It looks like the only thing we have going for us so far is that not all of them will have to be defeated by us. Three more of the infected birds turn on each other in a bloody battle, falling into the garden area and blasting each other with lightning. I won't complain. They can do us the favor and take each other out.

"What about ice? Like we did back on Crimson Isles?" I ask Soren.

"The wind is too strong." He grunts as he takes on the nearest bird in flight. Lightning riddles the ground around us, and everyone is jumping to get out of the way.

With a well-placed fire lasso around the bird's beak, he tugs and brings the bird to the ground. Jesse places an illusion around us, and we're able to keep the bird still long enough for Soren to deliver a blow to its chest.

The pitiful wail that leaves its beak makes my heart heavy.

It wasn't the creature's fault for being infected and going mad.

But this is giving me the time that I need.

Before Gideon was removed as headmaster, we trained on using water magic so that I could better learn to control it in the form of ice. I naturally evolved to that point when fighting off the first of the harpy eagles. And now that I'm free of my conduit, I'm confident I can use this skill even more effectively.

I close my eyes and feel the wind and rain. As soon as my energy is aligned with the very storm the harpies themselves created, I pull the water from the air and toward me, creating a vortex of water. With the moisture collecting around me, my body becomes chilly, nearly icy as the cooling magic in my veins takes over.

I pull all of that into me. Ice coats my arms and fingers as I aim for the next creature causing destruction to my home.

"Guys, duck!" My power may be amplified now, but precise aim is something I still need to practice.

As soon as they all turn to look at me, expressions an equal mix of confusion and worry, I let lose my magic. It fires true, coating the harpy eagle in a thick sheet of ice, freezing it solid.

Like a missile, the frozen creature falls to the

ground. Once the now bird-shaped icicle hits the ground, it shatters into millions of pieces.

Soren, Jesse, and Savannah stand up from the ground and stare at me in awe.

Jesse's expression is the first to turn into a proud smirk. "Quite the enigma, our woman."

Soren sets his shocked expression on Jesse as he steps toward me. "Are you okay?"

I nod. "Yes. I think so. But…"

"But what?" He leans in closer.

"I'm not wearing my conduit."

He nods. "Good. Keep doing it."

I nod, albeit a little shocked he took the news so easily, and prepare to pull the energy again. This time, I find my magic does it willfully, carefully. I smile as I feel like I'm in tune with it now more than ever.

One by one, I continue to freeze each of the plague infested creatures until none are left in the sky and the clouds are starting to part. The destruction has stopped on the castle, and my men and my friend are safe. But I'm freaking exhausted.

To push out that much power has taken its toll. And I know we are nowhere close to being finished with the fight. There's still Agatha, Westbrook, and that sniveling cook to take care of.

I slowly catch my breath as I spin in a circle, taking

in all the destruction and damage to not only my home but the grounds as well. Death is everywhere.

Soren and Jesse join my side, looks of concern on each of their faces.

"I'm fine," I say.

Jesse snorts. "That's cute."

"Yeah right," Soren adds.

I stand a little straighter and stare each of them in the eyes. "This isn't over yet."

"You got that right," Headmaster Westbrook says from behind us. "Professor McCallister, I need you to join the others in the clean-up efforts or in the stronghold."

Jesse chuckles at the headmaster's swollen face and burnt clothing. "Looks like someone's having a bad day."

I inwardly groan. "Soren, he's with the Order. I just barely escaped him."

A dangerous glint flashes in Soren's eyes. He steps forward, right hand filling up with powerful fire magic. As soon as he takes another step, he releases a fireball at Headmaster Westbrook's feet. "I hope you have made peace with your maker. You're about to meet him soon."

Westbrook smirks, unfazed by Soren's threat. "You're in no position to make such a move."

Agatha rushes out from one of the entrances, pointing a finger at me. "She used magic without a conduit! I saw it!"

"Your point is?" Soren asks, already blazing his hands up with fire magic.

Caseus shows up as well, though he's still wary of another attack. I can see that he quickly bandaged his injured arms, and he scowls at me as he joins the headmaster.

Agatha glares at Soren. "No wonder she attacked me in the common room. She's clearly crazy from using magic without a conduit. She's going dark. That means she has to die!"

A glowing red dot starts to pulse beneath Agatha's shirt. I narrow my eyes on her as she smiles wickedly. I know what that means. Milo is on his way. I absolutely cannot let that happen.

Somehow, I need to get that necklace off her and destroy it before Milo kills himself trying to traverse through all this mess.

"You'll pay for what you did to Milo," I warn her.

She chuckles. "What in the world are you talking about?"

Oh right, sure. Play coy.

Soren and the headmaster start to fight, magic erupting between them, while I keep an eye out for

Milo. I see him, and my heart aches for him. He's like a walking skeleton wrapped in skin. There's hardly anything of him left and I worry that we're already too late. The cook tries to toss in a cheap shot toward me. Jesse jumps in and blocks the attack. Savannah joins him, leaving me to face off with Agatha. Preferably before Milo gets here and struck by a deflected lightning bolt.

I narrow my eyes at her. "You're killing him."

"Well, someone is going to die. Leave him to me. He's no longer your concern."

Magic fills my hands. I'm done playing games. I'm done with threats. Time to end this.

She laughs. "Oh, you're going to love this next part."

I shake my head. "You're right."

I shoot a ball of fire at her, hoping to land a true shot and end this quickly. But she sees it coming, quickly dodging the blast as it hits the ground and sends mud, grass, and blood from the giant birds into the air.

That was a good move. Even for her. She learns quick for someone who prefers to run and hide.

Milo arrives as she pulls herself up from the ground. He looks at her obediently as she dusts herself off from the mud and grass that collected on her from rolling on the ground. She meets Milo's gaze with a satisfied smirk. "Kill her for me?"

He simply nods and takes a step toward me, magic filling his bony fingers.

I stand there, defiant and search Milo's eyes, knowing he's still in there, somewhere.

Savannah, within my periphery, sends a blast toward Caseus and sends him flying backward and crashing into a pile of rubble. This time, he doesn't move or get back up. She turns her attention toward me and Milo. Shock fills her eyes as she takes in the magic filling his hands, aimed at my chest.

"Milo! What are you doing?" she cries out.

Jesse starts to step forward, magic flowing in his hands. Keeping my eyes on Milo, I raise my hand in a gesture that demands he steps down. "No, don't."

Though the headmaster took cover behind a large rock during his fight with Soren, he sees what Agatha is trying to do and laughs. Soren aims another fireball toward him, making sure he doesn't dare come forward or try to jump into this tense moment.

As I stare at Milo, I try to figure out just how much magical energy he has left. Is he strong enough to kill me with a blast? I'm hoping there is a shred of my Milo left inside this worn-out frame. I need to know if there's enough of him left to see reason, that there is still fight left in him, and that a part of him is still hanging on.

As he approaches me, his hands take on an eerie green glow. He stops the moment he's three feet from me, staring at me with dark, lifeless eyes. His features scrunch like he's enduring intense physical pain.

Despite the voices of Jesse, Savannah, and Soren crying out to me, warning me to erect a shield, or get out of the way—I just can't. I tune out their voices. This is my Milo. He could never truly hurt me.

I step forward, slowly.

I'm so close to his glowing hand, that the heat of the magic is slightly burning my chest, right over my heart.

Agatha screeches. "Do it, Milo! Do it now!"

"I love you," I say in a clear voice, though my legs feel wobbly and my stomach is doing flips. "Do you hear me, Milo? I love you."

I stare into his vacant eyes, demanding that he hears my words and understand them. That they pass through the interference of the curse and reach his mind, and his heart.

Because if he doesn't hear me out, within the next few seconds, I'm going to have a burning hole in my chest.

CHAPTER TWENTY-FIVE

I don't need to get into a fighting stance.

I don't have to erect a shield or prepare a ball of fire. I just need Milo to look at me, listen to me, and respond.

"If you don't feel the same way," I say with a tremor in my voice, "then do it. Kill me."

He lets out a gasp at those words.

For the first time since that day in the hallway, I see that spark of light in his eyes. He groans as his body is thrown into a convulsion, his arms and legs jerking as if he's a marionette puppet.

I huff a breath of relief, realizing that he's actually trying to fight back against the curse. The green glow of the magic swirling in his hand flickers and fades.

Blood trickles from his nose as he finally drops his hand.

My gamble has won. He's still there. I just don't know for how long.

"Wren?" He shudders and doubles over, heaving as if ready to hurl. He lifts his gaze and gives me an apologetic look. That one look sends my heart soaring. It's all I need. "Wren… I'm sorry."

This is Milo. The real one. He's still in there, and he's still fighting.

I smile, even though tears sting my eyes and my heart is pounding in my chest.

I switch my gaze from Milo to Agatha. "There's not a curse in the world that can take him away from me."

"That's impossible!" she whines. "That's not fair!"

Oh, she has no idea yet what *fair* is. But that's okay, I'm about to show her.

Agatha looks like her head is about to explode. I want to revel in this moment, but it will have to wait. Things are about to get a little hairy.

Just as my hands light up with magic, a blast from Headmaster Westbrook sends all of us flying sideways, even Agatha. We all roll across the ground in different directions. I jump back to my feet, ready to rain hell on the headmaster and the spoiled brat.

"Get Milo out of here!" I shout to Jesse.

"I got him," Savannah says, grabbing onto him and pulling him toward the nearest castle entrance.

From the corner of my eye, Soren and Jesse also prepare their magic, ready to join in. I don't blame them. If it's one thing I've learned, it's that the Order never fights fair. They fight dirty, and they'll cheat to get their way.

Just like the trolls.

Agatha stumbles toward a chunk of tower lying on the ground. She's not going to hide again that easily. I chase her, but she quickly turns around and lets loose a small ball of white light. It hits me in the gut much quicker than I expected. I fly back, sky flashing through my eyes as I land hard on the ground and a piece of debris from the castle feels like it lodges into my back, square between my shoulder blades.

That was a cheap shot.

I'll give her props for that one, but that's about all she's going to get from me. As I quickly climb to my feet, I see Soren and Jesse taking on Headmaster West-brook. My men work seamlessly together to shatter the man's shield. My own shield bursts forth, and I am covered in fire. The flames dance along my skin as I stare at the woman responsible for Milo's condition. I once warned her to back off or deal with me... she didn't listen. Now it's time to pay the price.

"Give up now," I say.

"Why? So you can gloat?" Agatha's voice is so high-pitched it's irritating my ears. She launches another attack, this one bigger than before.

I deflect it easily with my shield and launch an attack of my own, sending a blast of fire hurling toward her. She dodges out of the way, surprisingly nimble for a girl that's been catered to most of her life.

It has to have something to do with that necklace.

To test this theory, I get closer to her. Thankfully, my magic doesn't react, but it doesn't necessarily disprove my theory as well. Something has happened to Milo, and if that crystal does what the curse states it does, that's the only explanation that fits.

Agatha tries to take a swing at me. I dodge the hit and land a kick to her torso. She bowls over with a grunt, leaving me the perfect opportunity to ram my knee into her nose.

She falls back to the ground, and I pace around her.

"All this time you thought you were free from the consequences of your actions? You thought you were winning Milo over, yet you remain blind to the fact that you're killing him."

"You don't deserve him," she mutters as she rolls to her hands and knees and struggles to climb to her feet and regain balance.

"And you do?" I ask.

Soren's fire magic catches my attention, and I take a few steps back to glance over and check on him and Jesse. Both of them are fighting brilliantly. They seem evenly matched at least with the headmaster, but I have a feeling the tides will turn in their favor soon.

At least they are keeping Westbrook busy while I settle this little issue of mine.

Agatha tackles me in the prime moment available to her. I silently curse at myself for becoming distracted by checking on my men. But just because she got the upper hand on me this time, doesn't mean she's dominating this fight.

She punches the crap out of my face, running through her energy like the untrained brat she is. I buck her off, sending her rolling over my head. I roll away to climb to my feet. Blood dribbles down my mouth from my nose with the few good hits she got in.

I hope she enjoyed it, because she won't be given any more.

I point my finger at her and let loose a bolt of pink lightning from my fingertips. She manages to dodge the attempt and land on her feet again. That amulet is burning brighter than ever, forcing me to check and make sure Savannah got Milo a safe distance away.

With the quick glance I allotted myself, she has. And that makes me relieved.

My plan is to wear her out. Make her yield and give her the chance to see the error in her ways. I'm honoring what I was told about her. That a little push in either direction was all it could take to swing her toward light or darkness. Gideon taught me that, and he is the greatest mage I look up to, besides Lady Alene. As much as I despise Agatha, even Gideon would give her a final chance. It's obvious Headmaster Westbrook and the cook manipulated her for their own ends.

She's not completely dark. Not completely lost, and I don't intend to kill her if she can see that.

I highly doubt she will. But for sake of the good in all people, I'm going to try.

"You'll never have him back. It's too late." Agatha laughs maniacally. "You're too late."

I try not to show her any reaction, but my emotions sometimes get the better of me. "For your sake, I hope that's not the case."

"What are you going to do about it?" she taunts. "Flash your stolen magic some more? At least I have pure natural talent."

"How do you know mine isn't?" I ask, pretending like the truth is beyond me.

"Caseus, duh." She saunters from side to side, matching my own movements. She wipes the blood from her mouth and winces as she rubs her broken nose. "He gave me an opportunity I couldn't refuse."

Oh, this I'm dying to hear. "And you ate right out of the palm of his hand?"

"No. Eww." She shivers like the idea really does disgust her. But I wasn't speaking literally. "He promised me everything I could ever want, as long as I got you alone and they were able to take what you stole from them."

I roll my eyes, sick to death of hearing that lame excuse. "Yeah, sure."

Agatha charges me. I lift my left hand and blast the ground at her feet, stopping her in her tracks. She damn near falls flat on her face trying to maintain her footing on slick grass. I almost chuckle at that.

"Ready to give up?" I ask.

"Never." She launches a fireball at me.

I dodge the blast easily and launch my own. But mine is bigger, hotter, and no way in hell is it going to miss.

I shoot my fireball toward her, anticipating she will dodge or jump out of the way. As she makes her move, I immediately extend my hand, sending forth a crackle of lightning that strikes her in the chest. Her eyes grow wide with the realization that she's met her end. The light leaves her blue eyes, and she slumps to the ground.

I let out a breath, slowly approaching her.

Kneeling next to her, I search for the necklace. In scanning her body, I only find the delicate chain barely dangling around her neck. I quickly search the ground surrounding her and find glittering red shards scattered throughout the grass.

The necklace is destroyed.

Finally.

But I have more to do to save Milo. We're not out of the woods yet.

CHAPTER TWENTY-SIX

"Perhaps... we can come to an understanding," the headmaster says, gauging his predicament. Westbrook flashes an uneasy smile, and he holds his hands up in surrender. "I can give the magusari names, intel... whatever they want. I'm more valuable to them alive."

Jesse shakes his head. "Nah. My vote is for the headmaster to die in an unfortunate accident."

Westbrook eyes me, slowly lowering himself to his knees and placing his hands on the ground, palms down. "Wren, I'm surrendering. Would you kill a prisoner?"

Finally, the jerk calls me by my name.

"Besides," Westbrook adds, "You're all tired out from fighting those harpy eagles, aren't you?"

I spot tendrils of black mist travelling across the ground.

"Watch out!" I shove Soren out of the way and one of the tendrils wraps around my leg, I scream out in pain, because it feels like I'm being electrocuted.

Several other black tendrils snake their way toward Jesse and Soren, and they dive out of the way, blasting at them with their magic. I fill my hand with a ball of fire and smash it against the tendril that has a hold on me. It shrivels and turns to dust.

Soren stands tall and releases his magic on Westbrook. The headmaster switches from his tendrils in order to parry the attack with his own blast. Looks like we're not the only ones tired. The headmaster can't use his tendrils and defend from blasts at the same time. I take advantage of this and lift my hands, adding the weight of my own blast of white light. Jesse joins in, and together, the three of us form a stream of bright energy that overpowers the headmaster's magic.

"No!" he screams out, just as our combined blast destroys his, leaving him defenseless. We take him down, obliterating every last physical ounce of him into nothing but dust.

"Wren!" Savannah calls out, and I desperately turn my gaze in the direction I heard her voice come from.

I rush over to the interior of the castle, with Jesse and Soren in tow. When I find her, my breath stills. Beside her, slumped on the floor in the hallway, lays Milo, face down.

Savannah runs a trembling hand through her hair. Tears spill from her eyes. "I tried to take him to the infirmary, but he just collapsed."

I kneel next to him and check for a pulse. Good, at least he's still alive. "I destroyed the necklace when I killed Agatha. There's nothing left of it. He should be revived."

Did I make a mistake? Am I too late?

Soren scoops Milo up into his arms. "He's fading."

"Not good," Jesse says, a look of worry in his eyes.

"Jesse and I gathered the supplies for the blood oath," Savannah says. "But the lab is destroyed so we had to set everything up in the infirmary."

The fall of footsteps catches my attention, and I turn to see Professor Crosswell running down the hall toward us. "Hurry," she says, almost breathless. "We don't have much time."

Soren nods, holding onto Milo for dear life. He follows Crosswell toward the infirmary, and the rest of us are on his heels.

When we arrive, half the place is littered with debris and the window is gone, but at least there's a bed free for Milo. As promised, Professor Crosswell has helped set up everything.

"Savannah, get the jar and knife," the professor says, rolling up her sleeves. Savannah rushes over to a nearby stand and grabs a jar of a paste like substance and a knife.

She approaches and holds them toward me. "All it needs now is your blood."

I look to Jesse and Soren. They nod once.

I take the knife while Savannah sets the jar of paste between me and Milo.

"Left hand. It's closer to the heart," Savannah adds.

I nod and run the blade over my left palm. I hiss a little at the sting. Dark blood pours out from the wound and I hold my clenched hand over the paste. "How much?"

Savannah hesitates a moment. "As much as you can feasibly give. Probably until the wound starts to clot."

"You're not sure?" I ask, horror rising in my voice.

"There weren't explicit instructions to amounts. This was mostly guess work here. But I'm positive what we have will do."

I nod, breathing out slowly while the blood slowly trickles to a stop.

"Here," Professor Crosswell holds out a cloth.

I take it and wrap it around my hand. "Now what?"

"Use your index finger and your middle finger only. Mix the blood into the paste."

I do, and the paste feels grainy and porous. My blood does little to thin the mixture, which I assume is a good sign. Once it's all mixed, I set my gaze on Savannah, who's holding up a picture of a transmutation symbol. Or, at least, what looks like some weird form of one.

It's of an hourglass shape. The corners on each side of the hourglass is joined by a line with a diamond parallel to the pint at the center of where the top and bottom of the hourglass meets.

"Draw this carefully over his torso," Professor Crosswell says as she points at the symbol. "Savannah, hold it still."

"Trying!" she says.

I take a calm, steadying breath. One small mistake could be the thing that either makes or breaks this ritual, and considering Milo's life is on the line, I can't allow for a single stroke to be out of place.

Dipping my fingers into the mixture, I draw the first line of the symbol, the top of the hourglass. I take another breath and carefully draw the first of the "X" shape. Once the hourglass is complete, I stretch out my neck to ease the tension in it and my shoulders and continue on to the diamonds and final lines to seal in the shape.

"Now what?" I ask.

"Now," Savannah says, setting the image of the transmutation symbol down. "Hold your left hand over the symbol and say these words." She holds up another page, words written on them.

I nod and read the incantation out loud. "My blood is your blood. I pledge myself to you. This unbreakable bond, I make to you. My blood is your blood. Let it be true. Nothing in this life or the next, can this bond undo."

A beautiful golden light emerges from my hand and fills the symbol on Milo's chest. Stinging shards stab through my hand and I struggle to keep my hand over his chest. The sensation is painful, uncomfortable and I desperately want to pull my hand back.

I clench my jaws and my right hand, standing there as it feels like my soul, at least a piece of it, is breaking away to join Milo's.

The agony of this ritual feels like it has been going on forever, even though only a couple of minutes pass. Before much longer, the pain starts to ebb and the light dies.

I collapse against the side of Milo's bed. Jesse and Soren instantly rush to my side. "I'm fine."

"She's hilarious," Jesse says to the room.

I focus on taking deep breaths as I feel the bond of the blood oath coursing through him. Setting my gaze on Milo's sleeping face, I can already see the color is returning to him.

"It's going to be a while before he wakes up," Savannah says. "We were almost too late."

I nod. "Thank you for all the help."

A series of nods roll through the room, and I notice Professor Crosswell walking toward the other end of the infirmary, where it seems a mini-lab has been set up. I purse my brows, leaving Milo's side long enough to figure out what is going on.

As I get closer, I notice all of her samples, including a few new ones are sitting on the surface. She gets down to business, immediately working on them.

"What are you doing?" I ask.

"In case you've forgotten, the plague is airborne."

Jesse joins my side. "And?"

Professor Crosswell stops what she's working on, sighs, and turns to face us. "We just fought a bunch of infected harpy eagles and their dead bodies litter most of the island and campus itself. By my estimation, many of us have contracted the plague and will start showing symptoms within five hours."

"Shit." That's not good. "Tell me you have found a cure."

I sincerely hope I didn't just go through all this mess only to wind up dying and leaving Milo to succumb to the plague after barely making it through the curse.

Professor Crosswell gives me a pointed look. "My dear, I did not come this far just to die of a cold from an over-sized bird."

Neither did I.

CHAPTER TWENTY-SEVEN

As the final effects of the blood oath takes hold, I can already see a real improvement in Milo.

I sigh in relief, falling into the chair at his bedside and resting my head on the edge of his mattress. The relief is short-lived, though. I watch Savannah and Professor Crosswell rush back and forth, almost crashing into each other, as they finish their final tests of the samples.

Five hours.

Within that time, we'll see whose skin grows pale and who starts coughing up blood.

Even worse, everyone is still crowded together down in the stronghold. We had sent Soren down to let the professors know what was going on, and he optimistically told them that Professor Crosswell already has a cure and would bring it down soon. At first, I questioned why he told them that, but then realized if they knew we only *might* have come up with the cure, then all hell would break loose.

I glance at Jesse and Soren still standing a few feet from the foot of Milo's bed. They look tired, exhausted. Soren has a few black marks on his cheek under his left eye. His focus is on Milo, watching as his chest smoothly raises and lowers more evenly as his breathing turns to normal as well as the color returning to his skin.

Jesse stands with his arms across his chest, also watching Milo. Relief fills his steel blue eyes.

Savannah finally comes over and takes the jar of what is left of the paste and sets it on a tray near the stand. She faces everyone with hope glowing in her amethyst eyes. "I'll be back with some food and water —at least, whatever I can scavenge—in case he wakes up. But like I said earlier, don't hold your breath. Although he's already showing some improvement, it may still be a while before he wakes up. My guess is it will take a few days. But, really, it's a waiting game until he does."

I nod. "Thank you."

She smiles. "Of course." Her voice is soft. She turns and grabs the tray, heading out of the room.

"Yes!" Professor Crosswell says from across the room. She's hunched over, and by the looks of it, looking into her microscope. "Yes, yes, yes."

"You did it?" Soren asks, joining the professor. "You found the cure?"

She turns to face him. "We won't know for sure until we test it, but if my calculations and observations are correct? Yes. I would test it first on one of the infected harpy eagles, but they're all dead."

Almost as if in response, a strange, high-pitched screech echoes through the broken window.

My eyes widen. "Not this shit again."

I stand from the chair and move toward the window. Outside, in the grass, frantically tugging at the chain still laced to its collar is Herbert. Somehow, likely through the destruction of the castle, he escaped.

He's acting weird though. Erratically moving and clawing at the chain. He's showing the same symptoms as the other harpy eagles. He's angry and he's out for blood.

"Well, I never thought I would ever say this," I say as I continue to watch the erratic movements of the giant bird, "But thank the gods Agatha kept this one locked up. Didn't seem to do much good, since he still got the plague. Still, this works out for us."

"Help me capture and contain him," Professor Crosswell says. "I will need to inject him with this and see if it works. If it's a success, I'll administer this to everyone here."

Here we go again. "Who's joining me?" I ask.

"I'll stay and keep an eye on Milo," Savannah says. "I've had more than my fill of those creatures. Besides, if he wakes up, you'll be the first to know." She smiles.

"All right, let's go." Jesse snaps his fingers and points to the door as he marches toward it.

I shake my head as I follow my men out the door. Like he always says, challenge accepted.

We made our way to the giant, afflicted bird in record time.

"Careful not to kill him," Professor Crosswell says.

We nod and quickly come up with a plan.

"How are we going to trap him and keep him calm long enough to administer the antidote?" I ask.

Jesse smirks. "That's my specialty."

Soren nods. "Good. You set up the illusion. Wren, you form a barricade of ice, like you did on Crimson Isles. I'll carefully hold onto the collar and keep him from snapping at Sarah."

Both Jesse and I nod.

Professor Crosswell crosses her arms, the needle

filled with our hope of a cure dangling from her nimble fingers. "You make it sound so easy."

"Trust us," Soren says.

"I'm very good at illusions, Professor," Jesse adds.

She frowns but nods in agreement. "Very well. The sooner we can get this done the better."

Jesse doesn't need more of an invitation. He approaches the bird, keeping a short distance from him. Soon, I see the glittering wall of an illusion taking place and the bird anxiously flaps his wings as it starts to fill his vision. It's freaking him out.

I'm not sure of how solid our plan is until the bird looks around him and eventually calms down. His breathing is erratic as his beak remains partly open. He scans the space in front of him, taking in some delightful vision only he can see.

I look at Soren, waiting for the cue. He nods. I face the bird and try to follow the same steps as before. Pulling the moisture out of the air, I dip into my magic and feel for the ice that starts to slowly grow within me.

The first time I did this was a fluke, the second—while training with Gideon—failed. This time, the fate of everyone on this island depends on this working.

Ice fills my veins, chilling my nerves and my arms start to feel heavier as I left my right hand toward the bird. Walking in a slow arc, getting as close as I can, I focus on forming a wall of ice similar to the one I did completely by chance back on Crimson Isles. Slowly, but surely, ice bleeds from my palms.

I surround the bird in ice, with a small opening to allow Soren and the professor through, complete with a roof to keep him from flying off.

Once I drop my hand, I let out a breath of relief.

Jesse winks at me. I smile.

A painful squawk comes from the ice dome and I snap my attention toward the doorway wondering if I should run in, preparing to fight another of the damned birds for the umpteenth time it seems. But seconds later, Soren and the professor walk out.

"Now, we wait," the professor says.

CHAPTER TWENTY-EIGHT

T he cure worked.

Thank the gods.

One week has passed, and it seems Blackbriar is still in recovery mode. Much of the castle has been repaired, though certain areas are still off-limits. The dead harpy eagles have been removed and incinerated, and everyone inoculated from the plague. Professor Crosswell is a freaking rockstar. Her vaccine has been distributed with lightning speed to both human and mage communities affected by the plague. She definitely came through, and it makes me even more determined to learn all I can from her.

Despite these little victories, there is still the issue of Agatha's death, of the demise of Caseus the cook, and of Headmaster Westbrook. Which is why I'm nervously standing outside of the council's meeting hall, trying to remain calm and remind myself that I did nothing wrong.

Well, except break into the restricted section of the library. But if they don't bring it up, I won't either.

I don't like being here, so far away from Milo, but this is for the sake of setting the record straight and clearing Gideon's name. We need to prove to the council that the Order's members had infected their ranks. This is also the final determination meeting.

Though Crimson Isles continues to enchant me, I'm unmoved by the clean, sterile atmosphere of the waiting area outside the doors to the meeting hall. Everything is a brilliant shade of cream stone, with rivers of silver and gold flowing throughout. The only hint of color is in the dark cherry stained wood benches and chairs that fill the space. Everything echoes. The soft whisper of my footsteps loudly carries through the air as I pace, waiting for my men to show up.

Finally, my men arrive, walking through the door. Soren and Gideon are in their formal best. Both wear black slacks and shoes. But Gideon wears a dark blue long sleeve button up and a black tie, and Soren wears all black with a dark silver tie. Jesse is in his typical jeans and t-shirt, with rips in the knees and just below his front right pocket. I take in each of them, delighting in how my magic's reaction flows through me.

As I bite the corner of my lower lip, I meet each of their gazes. My lips stretch into a wide smile as each of them look at me with love and desire.

These men of mine, I swear.

As they finally join me, each one takes a turn giving me a hug. Even Gideon, who goes last.

"Ready for this?" I ask him.

He shrugs. "As ready as I'll ever be."

"Let's not keep them waiting then," Jesse says.

Soren looks at him with a reproachful expression. He meets my gaze. "And you think I'm bossy?"

I chuckle. "You're rubbing off on him."

Soren takes the lead, huffing as he shakes his head, but I catch a glimpse of the smile he tries to hide, and I know he's not fooling anyone. Holding open the door, we file through into a room that starkly contrasts with the waiting area.

The walls are covered in portraits of past members, honored by deeds done in their service to the mage community. They encircle the room, starting with the first members of the first council all the way up to present. Beneath the faces permanently watchful of all the goings-on in this room is a rounded, half-circle set of raised seating. Each holds a member who patiently watches as we enter and take a seat behind a divider wall broken by a space large enough to walk through. Their expressions are a mixture of intrigue, accusation, and suspicion. All of them wear black robes with golden stoles around their necks.

A podium stands in the center of the floor between the two spaces. If the council wanted anyone who approached them to feel small, that would certainly do the job.

The door opens behind us. All of us turn to find my father, as himself, walking forward with Captain Lionel Rhodes by his side. He nods in greeting to the council and takes a seat behind us. I smile at him as he sets his gaze on me.

He smiles back.

It's comforting to have him here, but nerve wracking at the same time. But he promised me he has good reason, and all will work out.

I sure hope he's right about that.

I nod to the captain in greeting. He kindly returns the gesture as he takes his own seat.

"Welcome mages and magusari. The council is ready to hear your record," a member of the council sitting in the center says. He's one of the ones that had

a look of intrigue. I recognize him from the huge celebration we held for Lady Alene months ago.

Gideon nods and stands from his seat. As he
approaches the podium, he also nods to the council.
"Members of the council, it has come to my attention,
through formal investigation, that members of the
Order have not only been influential in the decisions
made in this council over the last few months—and
gods know how long—but also were behind the attack
on Blackbriar."

"Preposterous," one man with a long, dark beard
says.

"Where is your proof?" A woman asks. She looks
down her nose at Gideon with an accusatory glare.

A gavel slams against a block of wood, loudly
bouncing through the room. "We will hear everything
Mr. Storm has to say before falling apart." The same
man before looks at his counterpart members sternly.
Once everyone is silent, he nods for Gideon to
continue.

"Thank you, Chancellor," Gideon says.

Interesting. I didn't recall him being a chancellor,
but good information to know.

Gideon nods over to Soren, who pulls out a file
folder. He approaches the chancellor and hands him

the file. As the man opens and browses the collection of papers and photographs, Gideon continues.

"As you can see by the documents, photos, and sworn testimony of over fifty witnesses, the Order is not only alive and well, but bold enough to infiltrate the very heart of our community. Their members have harmed Blackbriar students, wielded their influence under the guise of being law-abiding mages, and are even responsible for the recent plague that overtook several cities."

The chancellor arches an eyebrow as he passes the papers and photos to his colleagues. Some of their expressions fall, while others look scandalized. However, the woman and bearded man scowl as if reading a ridiculous tabloid story.

Gideon clears his throat. "They will continue to do more, unless measures are put in place to prevent such actions. First, my former student, Wren Blackwood," he gestures to me, "was personally attacked by Deacon Lawrence just after her trials. It was then discovered that her father, once believed dead, was held captive by Mr. Lawrence who had charged him with finding pieces of a powerful artifact. Wren was used as leverage to keep Mr. Blackwood safe. He has since been rescued and cared for carefully since then."

The woman leans forward in her seat. "Yet, you

lied to everyone about Deacon Lawrence's death. You told the entire school he died fighting off a basilisk when he actually died by your hand. How can we believe you?"

"Council Member Grisolde," Gideon responds, eyeing her. "It is true I had to lie about the circumstances of Lawrence's death. I knew at the time I did not have a way to demonstrate to you all that I was, in fact, telling the truth regarding his motives and that of the Order. That is, not until today."

Lionel Rhodes stands and approaches with his own file. He hands it to Soren, who then hands it to the chancellor. Never once does Gideon's stare falter or his voice cracks. He's got this. "As you can see, chancellor and council members, Deacon Lawrence's ally within the Order, and his lover, was unfortunately Michael Blackwood's own sister, Patricia."

The chamber breaks out into murmurs. The chancellor views my father's information. "We shall enter into the record, Captain Rhodes' intelligence gathered."

"This is ridiculous," the council member with the dark beard says.

Protesting a little too much there, aren't ya?

A bald man, sitting next to Grisolde, rubs his chin. "Captain Rhodes trained under me. He's an honest and excellent magusari, as well as an expert in espionage. If he's gathered evidence supporting the connection between Patricia Blackwood and Deacon Lawrence, and their membership in the Order, then I'll vouch for it any day of the week."

Captain Rhodes smirks. "Besides, do you know how tough it is to get a statement from a troll? I had to wrestle three of them to assert my dominance, and then I drank their leader under the table to prove myself worthy in their eyes."

I quirk an eyebrow. That's not an easy task. Believe me. I've seen trolls drink themselves into oblivion before, and that took *days*. It's also horrible tasting stuff that reminds me of seaweed covered vomit mixed with leaves and dirt.

They had forced me to drink some of it solely to get a laugh out of my reaction. The taste stayed with me long after that, and I refused to give them the satisfaction of me drinking that foul stuff again.

Several of the council members break out into laughter. The chancellor covers his mouth with his hand to hide his own chuckle. He half-heartedly bangs his gavel. "Thank you, Captain Rhodes. We can see that the trolls corroborated the... arrangement they had with Patricia Blackwood."

As Gideon continues explaining everything,

including what transpired at Blackbriar with Head-master Westbrook and Caseus Demont, I take note of the council members, paying special attention to each expression. Some seem rather aggravated by the news Gideon is sharing with them, while others are listening intently, holding off on forming an opinion until the end.

I suspect there are no Order members here. Perhaps after hearing about what happened to West-brook at Blackbriar, they may have cut their losses and slipped away. The fact that three or four council seats are sitting empty has not escaped my attention.

Gideon pauses to take a deep breath. "Thus, ladies and gentlemen of the council, the attack on Black-briar, my removal as headmaster, and the threatened safety of all the students on the island was no accident or coincidence. All of these events have taken place over the course of several years. I have made numerous reports to the council, but the Order members who've weaseled their way in among you," he points toward the empty seats, "have either destroyed or altered my reports."

"Thank you, Mr. Storm," the chancellor says, "We also have yet to decide your continued placement as headmaster at the academy."

Gideon nods. "That is correct sir."

The doors to the meeting hall open abruptly. I barely turn around to see who's talking before an angry voice booms through the room. "I demand justice!"

Demitri Collins. Order member and father to Agatha, who fell by my hand.

Well, so much for this going easy.

The gavel slams against the wooden block as council members suddenly talk among themselves at the rude intrusion.

"I demand justice!" Demitri shouts once again.

The chancellor sits forward. "Mr. Collins, we are in a formal hearing. I insist that you go through the proper channels to stand before us. How dare you come in and demand anything from us."

He shakes his head, blonde hair a mess as he turns and points a finger at me. "This woman killed my daughter! I demand her immediate arrest!"

I gasp and look to Gideon, who seems less than thrilled about this man being here, and to the council who are now eyeing me with suspicion.

Getting accused of murder and potentially arrested is not how I thought this day would go.

Well, this just became a huge bag of fun.

CHAPTER TWENTY-NINE

"She killed my daughter! She's a murderer!" Demitri continues. He looks to Captain Rhodes. "Arrest her now!"

"I'm off duty and here by official request only," he responds with a shrug. "Sorry."

I smirk. Well, at least he's on my side.

"How dare you!" Demitri seethes.

Soren joins Gideon at the podium. "Council, if I may point out, Mr. Collins is the one who should be investigated and arrested. He sent his own harpy eagles to the island, which resulted in considerable damage to the castle and island as well as endangered the lives of everyone there."

"Chancellor," Gideon says before turning his gaze to the woman, "Council Member Grisolde. Your daughters are fine students at Blackbriar, and Demitri put them in danger.

"Chancellor," Soren adds, "your daughter's leg injuries. Did she tell you how they happened?"

"Yes. Debris from the castle fell on her, pinning her to the ground among other debris. She was in fear of her life. She credits you for her survival. And I thank you as well, Mr. McCallister, for running to her when she called for help. My daughter could have been eaten by one of those birds or crushed by another piece of falling debris." The chancellor chokes on his words and takes a moment to breathe. Once he regains his composure, he looks to Demitri Collins. "You will leave until it is your turn, submitted properly."

Demitri turns his anger filled gaze on me and he's seething. "I'll make you pay!"

He launches toward me, ready to claw out my soul.

I suck in a breath, muscles tensing.

Soren grabs the man before he can so much as even graze me with a fingernail, holding him back as Captain Rhodes approaches with some handcuffs dangling from his left hand. He sighs and shakes his head as Soren wrenches Demitri's hands behind him.

"Demitri Collins," the chancellor says, "You are

hereby placed under arrest for attempting to harm a witness to matter of the council."

Demitri growls and snarls like a rabid beast as the captain leads him out of the room.

He glares at me as he is led away. I feel for the man. I really do. But he is also responsible for his daughter's death. Not just me.

"Now that we've handled that," the chancellor pauses and states, "there is the matter of clearing Michael Blackwood."

My father takes a stand and submits all the papers and blueprints that he had been risking his life for. He gives them to the chancellor.

"Very well," the chancellor says. "We will review the evidence and reconvene shortly. We will also make a final decision regarding the reinstatement of Gideon Storm at Blackbriar Academy."

Everyone stands and slowly files out of the room, back into the plain waiting area while the council deliberates.

For now, this whole thing is out of our hands.

"Are you okay?" Soren asks.

I face him and nod. "Just anxious. I hate waiting."

He smirks. "I've noticed."

"Are you sure we're doing the right thing?" I ask.

"Yes." He rubs the tops of my arms with his hands. "Relax, this is a good thing."

I nod. But I can't help but worry. The backlash could be more than we expect, and uncovering the secrecy behind the Order will not go unpunished by its members.

"Gideon presented himself well. It was interesting to watch him deliberate with the council."

"That's because I have had a lot of practice," Gideon says, joining me at my right.

I smile as he rests a hand on my back. "I hope this won't take long."

I hate waiting.

He chuckles under his breath. "It won't."

I nod and excuse myself to go talk with my father for a moment. He seems lost in thought, and I worry about him too much sometimes. As I approach him, his attention snaps to me, and within seconds, his eyes relax into a smile hidden by his beard.

"Hey," I say.

"Hey," he chuckles. "What's up?"

I smile at his question and take a seat next to him on one of the wooden benches. "How are you holding up?"

He shakes his head, leaning forward on his knees, fingers tented between them. "It's been a long time since I've stood in this room. In this building. It's surreal."

I nod. "I bet it's a bit overwhelming."

"A little." He holds his finger and thumb up with a small space between them, squinting as he speaks.

"You're doing great, Dad." I pat him on the back.

Jesse walks up to us and settles for leaning against the wall, arms crossed over his chest. "Well if this ain't the greatest way to spend a Saturday, I don't know what is."

"It'll be over soon," I say.

A short while later the doors to the meeting hall open, and we all stand and make our way back to our seats.

Gideon retakes the podium and waits to be addressed by the chancellor.

"Gideon Storm, the council stands in a unanimous decision. As a student of Blackbriar, you have proven yourself as a worthy mage, making the right decisions and always leading others. It was that, and your excellent service as a magusari that led us to place you as headmaster of the academy. Though your indiscretion, which you have not denied, is a serious matter, your years of loyalty and service are simply unmatched by any other candidate. It is with great honor that we restore you to your position as headmaster."

I beam, bouncing in my seat. He did it! He got his job back.

Gideon grins, and his shoulders ease as he releases a breath.

"Council members, I'm honored for the opportunity to once again prove myself to you, but it is with regret that I must turn down your offer and pledge myself in other ways."

What!?

Murmurs float throughout the chamber as heads turn toward one another. This clearly wasn't the response they were expecting either.

"If I may ask, why?" The chancellor eyes him curiously.

"My relationship with Wren Blackwood is important to me, and I believe that my strengths would be better put to use in protecting the island from future attacks. I understand that I cannot have the Head-master position and her, and it would be unfair for me to be divided in such a way or to live a lie. However, two things I am certain of—I am dedicated to her, and I am dedicated to protecting Blackbriar."

"In what way?" The man's eyebrows draw close to each other and he seems to have a frown pulling at his lips.

Gideon nods. "I propose the opportunity to station

an outpost of magusari on the island. I can train and be the Commander of the Blackbriar Academy Special Forces. This will ensure we have an elite group of mages equipped to defend the school when the need arises. The safety of all students will be our priority. This also allows me to maintain my relationship with Wren, as well as play a more integral role on the island."

"Councilmen in favor?" Chancellor says.

The majority of hands raise into the air.

"All opposed?"

Very few hands raise into the air.

The gavel is slammed against the block. "The council approves of this movement. However, I highly suggest you choose your most trusted men to join you in this endeavor, as we are still cleansing the stain of the Order from among us."

"I will, Chancellor."

"If I may," the chancellor continues, "We request that Michael Blackwood step forward."

Gideon turns around and nods to my father.

My heart is racing and panic floods through me as I sit up straighter and watch my father approach the council.

"It is a pleasure to finally see you again, Mr. Blackwood."

"Thank you, Chancellor. The feeling is mutual." He bows slightly.

"I'm afraid your welcome back isn't going to be so smooth, however. Because of the events surrounding your perceived death, the time you spent in captivity with the Order, the transition back to life among us, as well as rebuilding your reputation, will take some time. It's not necessarily you specifically, but you come to us at a time where the Order has made an insidious infiltration of the magusari and of Blackbriar Academy. We must be cautious. Do you understand?"

My father's shoulders slump, and the breath leaves my lungs.

This is looking like it's going to go exactly how I didn't want it to.

"Mr. Blackwood, the council requires your continued cooperation with the investigation. That includes providing us the names of the ones you know are part of the Order, as well as any further intelligence you've gathered. We've authorized Captain Rhodes to work closely with you on this. Your help in bringing them down will earn your place back among us."

"Anything, Chancellor." My father bows slightly again.

The chancellor nods. "Now, are there any other

items to discuss?" He looks out over the room. Satisfied, he takes in my father. "I ask that you remain behind." He looks to Gideon. "Mr. Storm, I assure you that the council will fully investigate the most recent reports regarding the Order. You may begin your work at Blackbriar as soon as possible. We'll need it."

Gideon nods.

The gavel slaps the block twice, dismissing the hearing.

Before I follow the others out, I rush to my dad and give him a hug. "I love you."

He wraps his arms around me tightly and kisses the top of my head. "I love you too, little bird."

CHAPTER THIRTY

I t's been about two weeks since the attack on Blackbriar, and the cleanup is finally coming to a close. The repairs on the castle still have a little way to go, but the improvements have the towers, ceilings, and gardens looking as good as new.

We have one last batch of the cure saved for Savannah's father, at his request. We're at the docks waiting for Mr. Fey, sitting with our feet dangling over the edge and swinging them back and forth as we watch the waves roll in.

The roar of the boat's motor is heard moments before the thing itself comes into view. Savannah and I quickly jump up from the dock and slip our shoes and socks back on and hurry to the end of the docks to greet her father.

Savannah stands with her hands clasped in front of her, practically bubbling over in excitement at finally seeing her dad after quite some time.

A quite handsome man steps off the boat and immediately greets Savannah with a hug. I stand off to the side, watching happily as my best friend is finally reunited with her father. Once they separate, he faces me, and I see where Savannah gets her eyes from. Her father's amethyst eyes stand out against his short dark hair and full beard.

"You must be Wren."

I smile and nod. "That's me."

He holds out his hand to me. I set mine in his and he firmly clasps my hand, giving it a strong shake. "I'm Robert. Pleasure to meet you. I've heard quite a bit about you."

"Likewise, your reputation precedes you."

"Indeed." He smiles beyond his beard and I can see where Savannah also gets her charm from. "Well, I am here on business, so please lead the way."

I nod and take the lead, allowing Savannah to catch up with her father as we head toward the courtyard. There, we meet with Soren and Gideon. Once the pleasantries are out of the way, Robert makes his way up to the infirmary, where the samples he requested are stored in a secure box.

After collecting the box, he makes his way back down to us, with Professor Crosswell in tow, he faces Gideon. "I assume you still have the unaffected birds here on the island?"

"Yes. Follow me." He winks at me just before he turns and leads Savannah's father to the area of the island where the few still-living harpy eagles are.

"So, what do you think?" Savannah says as we follow the group.

"About?" I ask, playing coy.

"My dad... duh." She giggles.

I shake my head, laughing under my breath. A warm breeze brushes through my hair and I tuck it back and set my gaze on just how happy my dear friend is. "I think he's a charmer. I can totally see you get some of your most valued traits from him."

"I am a daddy's girl," she says proudly.

"He's very professional, too," I add.

"Oh, yes. But don't let that fool you, he's quite a bit like Jesse."

"Interesting." The man seems lighthearted for sure, but he certainly seems to have his priorities straight. He wouldn't strike me as the type to play pranks or not take things seriously.

We are the last to arrive on the sandy shore where the harpy eagles have been kept at a safe distance from the reconstruction efforts. These ones aren't so bad. They're trained. They're unaffected by the plague. They're the reason we have a cure. Good birds.

Robert, Soren, and Gideon stand at a distance from the birds, chatting with Professor Crosswell. As we catch up to them, I overhear the last of their conversation.

"That's right," Professor Crosswell says, "I've collected the specimens and tested them myself twice just a few hours ago. They remain clean. We won't have to worry about that plague ever again."

"Excellent," Robert says. "I appreciate you letting me have these extra samples. I'd like to see what other applications they have."

"If you don't mind, I've worked my tail off on this for the better part of the year. I would love to share my notes with you and aid in any way I can."

Robert smiles at the woman. "It would be my pleasure to have your help."

Professor Crosswell beams. "I'll get you my notes immediately. It's a pleasure to meet you."

"No, the pleasure is mine, Professor Crosswell. My colleagues are raving about you," Robert says.

Professor Crosswell excuses herself and quickly makes her way back up to the castle.

"What is going to happen to them now that you

have what you need to make a cure?" I eye the group of harpy eagles. They seem content.

"They'll be safe on my property," Robert says. "With all that's going on with the Collins farm, they'll need a home. At least, temporarily. In fact, I could use some help getting them loaded and transported," he says to Gideon.

"We will be happy to help with a couple of good men." Gideon turns and heads off to do that.

Meanwhile, Robert pulls out a tranquilizer gun and shoots a dart into each of the three giant birds, moving with a surprising amount of speed. Each of them startles at first, but quickly relax and fall to sleep on the sand. "They'll be out for the day. That should be long enough to get them back."

Soon the boat with the crazy captain shows up just off shore just as Gideon returns with a few of the beefiest men he could find. Once the birds are loaded up, Savannah says a short goodbye to her dad.

When she joins my side again, it's like a weight has been lifted from her shoulders.

"Feel better now that we have a cure?" I ask.

She sighs, watching her father shrink along the horizon. "Yeah. It won't be long now."

"Wren!" Jesse's voice calls to me.

I snap my attention toward him. He waves me

over. I roll my eyes and face Savannah once more. "Be right back. Mr. Boss requests my presence."

She chuckles. "Go on, I'll help wrap up everything around here."

"Thanks." I turn and head toward Jesse. I playfully take my time, laughing as he tries to get me to hurry up, gesturing a bit more urgently.

As soon as I'm within ear shot, he sighs. "Took you long enough."

I shrug. "Had to tease you in any way I could."

"Well, you're not just teasing me," he says.

I look at him puzzled. "What?"

"He's waking up, babe," he says. I think he was just playfully calling me babe, but it makes me smile almost as much as the news does.

"Race you." I take off without waiting for a response.

The halls breeze by me in a blur and I can't seem to get my feet to move fast enough for me to make it to the infirmary. This has been such a long wait, and I'm anxious to see him.

I round the last corner, already feeling the effects of Milo's magic reacting to mine in full force, leading to the infirmary and stop outside the door as I can see Milo sitting up in his bed, frowning. The moment gives me pause as I take a deep breath and step inside, slowly. I don't want to overwhelm him with my approach, especially since he just woke up from a coma.

I make it three steps in, and his gaze settles on me. His brown eyes lighten with joy. "Wren," he breathes. His lips stretch into a smile and I just can't contain myself.

I run.

I jump into the bed, wrapping my arms around him tightly. "I'm so glad you're okay."

He hugs me back. Just as tightly and doesn't even want to let me go so I can settle in next to him. Eventually, I do, and I rest my head on his shoulder.

"I thought I would never get to see you—the real you—again." My words come out low, so that I don't show too much emotion. Because any louder, I would cry.

"I didn't think I was going to make it either," he murmurs in my hair.

He kisses my hair and I angle my head to look deep in his eyes. "You'll have to do better than that," I say, smiling.

He chuckles and presses his lips to mine. Even despite the awkward angle, I feel him. The real him. Even my magic's reaction to him is in full force.

I'm so glad I can still kiss him.

I snuggle into Milo, breathing in deep his scent, not wanting this moment to end. We watch the sun slowly set along the horizon, as we sit on the beach of the island, and this moment couldn't be more perfect. More peaceful.

He wraps his arms tighter around me, leaving a kiss on the top of my head, and I just can't get enough of him right now. After nearly losing him completely, I don't want to spend a single moment away from him.

Call that what you will, but I don't ever want to take for granted that my men are bullet-proof. Especially from googly-eyed spoiled brats with a vendetta.

I really soak in this moment, enjoying the cool rush of my magic's reaction to him.

It's back, and it's better than ever.

"I never thanked you," he whispers.

"For what?" I ask.

"For saving my life. The risks you took, and for never giving up on me."

I twist to face him. He takes me into his deep brown gaze, and I'm so grateful to see the Milo I know and love reflected in them. "I don't know what to think yet about the Blood Oath, but I am very grateful you did it." His voice is soft, pensive almost.

"I would never give up on you. There aren't any lengths I wouldn't go to for you, Soren, Gideon, or Jesse."

"I hope you never tell him that, it'll make his head bigger."

I chuckle. "Probably. Let's just keep it between us."

"Seriously, though." He nudges me. "Thank you. I'm eternally grateful."

"Just don't go making impressions on any first year students from now on, okay?" I tease.

"You got it."

"Good." I smile.

He pulls me in closer. "Getting cold?"

"No, I'm perfectly comfortable."

He chuckles under his breath. "I feel like I've missed so much over the time I was not myself."

I shrug. "I know. But you'll catch up in no time."

"You have astounding faith in me," he says as his gaze settles on the last remnants of dying light.

"Well deserved faith," I correct. "If you need a study buddy, I'm your woman."

"That would be great."

We fall into a blissful silence and I just can't get enough of just being here with him. Just him and me. But soon, Gideon joins us, and we become a party of three.

"Hey, you," I say. "Pull up a piece of beach and join us."

He obliges with a smile on his face and settles in close.

"Any news?" I ask.

He slowly shakes his head. "Still waiting on word from my contact on one of the locations of the Order. But he did say it's safe to prepare to leave."

"Good."

We're taking the fight to them this time. No more surprises, and this time, we have an army of mages backing us.

"I'm glad you're feeling better, Milo."

Milo nods. "Me too, Gideon. Me too."

More steps crunch behind us, and with the heat burning through me, I know it's Soren. He takes a seat on the other side of Milo.

"'Bout time you joined us, slacker," I say.

He snorts. "Who's this?" He gestures to Milo.

"Very funny," Milo says.

It feels good to be able to tease each other and just enjoy this peaceful moment, soaking it up. Because soon, we'll be fighting the Order, and that's going to be a hard-won war.

"There you are!" Jesse says as he joins us, and my

team is finally whole again. "Didn't I tell you, there's no party if I'm not in it?"

I shake my head. "Just sit down and enjoy the moment."

"Yes, ma'am." He hams up a salute and plops to the ground, stretching out his legs in front of him, crossing them at the ankles and keeping himself propped up with his arms. He narrows his eyes on Milo. "Hey, stranger."

Milo half-asses a wave. It's sarcastic, and I love it.

My men give each other hell and I sit back and watch. This is something I don't think I will ever take for granted ever again. My men. My team. My family.

We belong together. We are stronger, more united, and forever changed for the better.

The Order has made their last attempt at taking my magic away. I will defeat them and dismantle their organization if it's the last thing I do. Because I know that is the only way they will leave me and my men alone.

I'm no longer playing nice.

They fucked with the wrong rose, and now they are going to get my thorns.

Wren, Soren, Gideon, Jesse, and Milo will be back in *The Battle of Blackbriar Academy,* coming soon!

Join the exclusive, fans-only Facebook group to get release news & updates.

Read on for a special note from the author.

AUTHOR NOTES

Hey, Babe!

Phewy! What a ride! My heart is still pounding! How about yours?

Thank you so very much for sticking with me this far on Wren's journey. It's been such a fun and fantastic adventure! But her story isn't over just yet.

Wren's third year certainly takes the cake. Don't you think?

In book one, she faced trials, and learned that nothing is going to stand in the way of her achieving happiness and a place to belong.

In book two, she rescued her father, defeated a zacar after her powers, and learned of the Order's intent on taking what she has.

In book three, she faces off with her aunt and

learns that the Order is going to stop at nothing to take her power away. But that's okay, she's *prepared*, and with her men at her side, nothing can stop her.

In this book, she realizes just how far the Order will go in order to rip away her power, up to and including removing her men in an attempt to make her vulnerable. Agatha teams up with the cook to steal Milo away, even to the point of endangering Milo's life. Gideon's position as headmaster is threatened. Soren has to keep a distance since he's a professor and the new headmaster doesn't care if Wren and Soren were together before he accepted the position.

Worst of all, the school she loves and calls home comes under attack by giant harpy eagles with storm magic. Just in the nick of time, she uncovers the deadly curse Agatha placed on Milo, how she was able to come across a spell no second-year student should be able to cast, and unravels the Order's plans of stripping Wren of her comforts and men.

She stops them all and saves Milo with the help of her men, Savannah, and Professor Crosswell's impeccable knowledge. Plus, they find a cure to the plague!

Take *that* Order!

I truly hope you join me on the next and final installment of the Blackbriar series. It will be the ultimate showdown, and Wren will blow your mind.

What final maniacal plan will the Order pull in order to get to Wren? And how do Milo and Wren adjust to the Blood Oath, now that they're bound for life? Will anyone else from Wren's past make an unexpected appearance?

You'll have to read the next book to find out!

Until next time, babe!
Keep on being your beautiful, badass self.
-Olivia

PS. Amazon won't tell you when the next Blackbriar Academy book will come out, but there are several ways you can stay informed.

1) **Soar on over to the Facebook group, Olivia's secret club for cool ladies,** so we can hang out! I designed it *especially* for badass babes like you. Consider this as your invite! We talk about kickass heroines, gorgeous men, our favorite fantasy romances, and... did I mention pictures of *gorgeous men?*

2) **Follow me directly on Amazon**. To do this, **head to my profile** and click the Follow button beneath my picture. That will prompt Amazon to notify you when

I release a new book. You'll just need to check your emails.

3) **You can join my mailing list by going to** https://wispvine.com/newsletter/olivia-ash-email-signup/. This lets me slide into your inbox and basically means we become best friends. Yep, I'm pretty sure that's how it works.

Doing one of these or **all three** (for best results) is the best way to make sure you get an update every time a new volume of the *Blackbriar Academy* series is released. Talk to you soon!

ABOUT THE AUTHOR

OLIVIA ASH

Olivia Ash spends her time dreaming up the perfect men to challenge, love, and protect her strong heroines (who actually don't need protecting at all). Her stories are meant to take you on a journey into the world of the characters and make you want to stay there.

Reviews are the best way to show Olivia that you care about her stories and want other people discover them. If you enjoyed this novel, please consider leaving a review at Amazon. Every review helps the author and she appreciates the time you take to write them.

www.ingramcontent.com/pod-product-compliance
Lightning Source LLC
Chambersburg PA
CBHW020529020726
47494CB00006B/1695